WHEN
butter*f*lies
KISS

(second edition)

D0814089

WHEN butterflies KISS

(second edition)

a serial novel by:

SékouWrites
Elizabeth Clara Brown
T'Kalla
Kiini Ibura Salaam
Korby Marks
Shange
Kim Green
Mariahadessa Ekere Tallie
Natasha Tarpley
Tish Benson

edited by:
SékouWrites

copy edited by Kenrya M. Rankin

Front cover design by
Sheri Collins

Front cover photograph by
Shadez Communications

ISBN: 978-0-6151-7220-0

Dedication

What happens to a dream deferred? It refuses to die. *When Butterflies Kiss* consumed my life for two years prior to its August 2001 release, but news of its debut was quickly buried under the much more pressing headlines of 9/11. Although this uniquely created novel went on to garner critical acclaim, it never quite found its sales stride before it went out of print in 2003. Years later, I still get emails from people who have randomly discovered *When Butterflies Kiss* and are moved by its (unintentional) message of black male self-discovery; these are the people who inspired me to revise and release a second edition of *When Butterflies Kiss*. Thanks to all of you.

Introduction

Let's pretend this is a magic show. The magician is about to perform his tricks and (hopefully) you'll be duly impressed. Will you be satisfied with the illusion or will you need to know the secrets? If you're the type of person who wants to know what's behind the veil in advance, skip to the end of the book now and read the collection of questions and answers assembled there. If, however, you're the type to be satisfied with the illusion, just keep reading.

The questions you'll find at the back of the book are designed to both elucidate the process behind creating a serial novel like *When Butterflies Kiss* and also give insight into the themes and characters of the story. So, even if you don't read it now, you'll want to read it after you complete the novel. I'm certain you'll be surprised by the answers.

Also, you'll notice that each new chapter has a title but no author byline. This is to ensure that you will not treat this work as a collection of individual short stories. Many readers of the first edition didn't fully understand that *When Butterflies Kiss* was a single, continuous narrative with multiple authors, so they skipped around, reading the chapters out of sequence. If you read it that way, though, you'll miss the magic. Don't worry, the author information for each chapter is printed at the back of the book.

One final note. I enjoyed the journey of *When Butterflies Kiss* as if I was a new reader who had nothing to do with its outcome because, in many ways, I was. Hope you enjoy the journey as much as I did.

Chapter One

The Midnight Ocean of Moonlit Rivers

"I'm in way over my head." That single thought rose through the brother's mind like a moan created in the first delicate moments of escalating passion. Seconds later, it exploded like a staccato sigh somewhere near the center of his expectations.

He shifted. Cradled the phone a little tighter into the crook of his shoulder. It wasn't what she'd said that moved him. Her exact words were already cloudy in the haze of his memory. It was the texture of *how* she'd delivered those words that had engulfed him powerfully; rushing through his mind with enough force to make him feel like a lone bead of sweat swallowed into streaming rivulets of passion.

His phone call had awakened her. She'd sounded groggy, disoriented, exhausted ... but that was before he said, "Hello."

"Hey, baby, I'm so glad you called." The sentence was a simple one; it was her inflection that made it extraordinary. Seven words. Only seven words. Yet in that short space she'd managed to float her voice smoothly through the muddled malaise of sleep, make a brief pit stop in the land of ebullient effervescence, and end in a lascivious come-hither intonation that commanded the hollow space in the pit of his stomach to tremble and swirl like a desperate leaf trapped at the tail end of a monsoon. He'd never heard a sister shift gears so fast.

Mid-sentence? Sister-girl was a pro.

When she'd answered the phone, he'd fully expected to get shot down from jump. When she told him to call her tonight ("no matter what time it is") he'd felt his spider-sense tingling— but, uh, it wasn't hardly tingling enough to keep him from calling. She was still sexy enough to give every brother in the club whiplash.

That, plus the agonizing fact that his long-term relationship had just dissolved days ago, made her attentions completely irresistible and right on time to distract him from heartache.

"Talk to me," she said. Her lilt throbbing low and cat-like, like she was just waiting for him to throw her a tinfoil ball of flirtation that she could bat about with her paws.

"Did you miss me?" He came with his deepest voice. Borderline Barry White. No harm in playing along, right? Even though he'd just met her a couple of hours ago.

"Did I *ever* … if only you knew how much." Her voice was killer. The kind of voice that phone sex empires are built upon. And it seemed like she'd already sized him up accurately. Figuring he wasn't gonna go for the hard-to-get routine, she was coming in low and fast, intent on making him believe that he was Mack Daddy Supreme and his every utterance was driving her wild.

Please, I've never had that much game in my life, he thought. But it sure felt good to pretend that she was succumbing to his seductive spell, so he let that last sip of vodka take control as he struggled to fit into the britches of his wannabe alter ego, Big Daddy Love.

"So, tell me," he said. Still deep, a little playful, trying hard to run the show.

"Tell you what?" She didn't quite see where he was going and he relished the small victory.

"Tell me … how much you missed me."

"Mmmmm … I could show you better than I could tell you." Trés sexy. As soon as she knew where he was headed, she upped the ante on him. The consummate seductress. He was loving every minute of his suddenly exciting life.

"I was hoping you'd say that, baby," he said, his voice sounding just as bedroom as hers. Of course, he'd been hoping no such thing. He was just fighting to hold up his end of the sexual repartee. Back in the real world, her suggestiveness had him pinned helplessly against the ropes. A fact that made itself plain as he noticed with embarrassment the stirrings that were beginning just below his belt.

"And why is that?" she asked, testing his mettle.

Uh-oh. "Because there are a couple of things I'd like to show you, too." Okay, not bad, baby-boy. Keep it up. And that wasn't so much of a stretch anyway. After the things she'd done to him at the club earlier that night—on the dance floor, no less—he did indeed have a few things he'd like to show her. He wanted to see if he could hem her up as bad as he'd been hemmed up earlier. He still couldn't believe he'd allowed that dance floor thing to happen in front of his ex-girlfriend but, hey, when opportunity comes knocking and ain't nothing else but heartbreak at your door … you'd be surprised at what you might do.

"Oh, *really*?"

"Yeah, really." He looked at his watch, calculating logistics. It was three in the morning. She'd said she lived about thirty minutes away. She'd been asleep. He'd just walked out of the party. In fact, he was still in the nightclub's lobby. A fact he was actively trying to keep her from getting hip to, lest he get lumped into the "naw-girl-he's-too-desperate" category. Just to make sure, he had halfway hidden himself behind an oversized column in case any of his homeboys saw him and decided to clown.

From what she'd said, the club was a lot closer to her apartment than his apartment, and he didn't want to go all the way home if this was gonna turn out to be the booty call he hoped it was. Course, he'd never made a booty call, so there was no telling if he'd be able to pull it off. Old girl was talking one hell of a game but he knew damn well it could be just that—a game.

"What kinda things?" she purred.

Hold up. The last time he'd told a sister *exactly* what he wanted to do to her—after hours of flirtatious prodding from her, mind you—he'd been introduced to Mr. Dial Tone faster than it took to realize he'd been played. Not this time.

"Uh … I could show you better than I could tell you," he said. She laughed lightly, apparently liking the fact that he'd turned her own game around on her, and he celebrated his narrow escape from hang-up hell. There was a pause as she settled back into the driver's seat.

"Do you want to fuck me?"

He almost dropped the phone. OhmyGod, he thought, desperately fighting to recover. Feeling confident in his last successful thrust and parry, he'd been completely unprepared for such a pointed attack. But, hell, there was no way in the world he'd have ever been prepared for that question. Good Lord. It was all he could do to stop himself from stammering out a, "What," and giggling like the village idiot until she let him off the hook. But then he realized that this was *it*. This was the test. He had less than a fraction of a second to nail this question—without appearing amateurish or making her feel objectified—or he was gonna find himself a honorary member of the Blue Boy Fingertip Quintet for the evening.

He opened his mouth, having no idea what he was about to say.

"I would *love* to make love to you."

"Ooh, shit." It followed his sentence so closely that he wasn't sure if she was responding to him, or some strange bump that she'd heard in the night. He hoped she was responding to him. He hoped he'd passed the test. When the pause became too pregnant to bear, he ventured out cautiously. "'Oh shit,' what?"

"I like that. What you said."

"Yeah?" He wasn't sure if what he'd said was truly enticing or if she was still playing him up to be super-mack-daddy but either way, it sounded like he was home free. He relaxed a little, noticing for the first time his white-knuckle grip on the cell phone.

"Oh, yeah ... " When she left it out there without elaborating he figured he was in the driver's seat again.

"And why's that?" There was a small puff of air that could have been a laugh in response. "Hmmm?" he prodded, beginning to enjoy the chase.

"Well ... " She was teasing now. He knew she wanted to tell him, wanted him to chase it out of her. He happily obliged.

"C'mon ... tell me."

"Well ... let's just say one of my pet names is 'the ocean.'"

Her phrase shared the sinister deception of a grenade thudding softly into the earth, coaxing you with momentary silence that it poses no threat at all. Then it laughs loudly, a booming chuckle with a thousand cotton balls of scorching flame tumbling behind it, snuffing out the light of everything close enough to feel its grin.

Did she just say 'the ocean'? Her verbal grenade finally exploded and the implications dawned on him—heavily. The stirrings below his waist shifted, gaining warmth and volume incrementally.

"Oh, really?" It was all he could think to say.

"Mmm-hmm ... and you just made quite a river."

She did not just say that. His thoughts reeled suddenly out of his reach, intently working and reworking multiple combinations and permutations where the river inside her ocean played dominatrix. Okay, keep cool, bruh. Don't trip ... but damn! He felt his jeans pulling tight as part of him sought out more space—making room to skinny dip in her midnight oceans and moonlit rivers. He took a breath, tried to regain focus. A line from one of his boy's pimp-ology manuals played in his head. "Close the deal, man. Just close the damn deal."

Pushing past the embarrassment of being stuck in the corner of a nightclub lobby until he could settle down enough to stop stretching his pants into dynamic new shapes, he pulled on every suave daddy vibe he had for the line he hoped would end the teasing.

"Yeah? So, what do you wanna do about that?" Delivered in his best Iceberg Slim, Superfly, Marvin Gaye "let's git it on" rumble.

"You tell me, baby." Voice like velvet.

"I can be there in five minutes," he lied.

"Yeah?"

"Yeah." He smiled into the phone. He'd had his doubts earlier, but now he was certain: he was about to get paid. He found himself fishing in his pockets for cash. Now, all he had to do was ditch his boys, catch a cab and —

"I can't let you fuck me," her sentence knifed swiftly through his mental victory dance and left his hope falling toward his feet in tatters. He stilled, staying silent and immobile while he nursed a belief that he'd heard her wrong — hoping that his sloshy fantasies of wading into her rivers-inside-oceans weren't about to dry and crack like parched riverbeds in the desert. But the belief drained out of him in a big dumping rush with her next words.

"My fiancé is coming back into town tomorrow."

Chapter Two
Dust

I t wasn't exactly a lie. Not exactly. And she didn't go out looking for a game. But men who believe they have been wronged cannot hear with both ears. And so she told the lie that wasn't exactly a lie (because she believed it was true), knowing in her heart that it would be the easiest truth to digest. For both of them.

Derek was her fiancé; he just didn't know it yet. And if he didn't come back tomorrow, he'd definitely come the next day. By the end of the week, at the very latest. He had to return soon. He'd been gone long enough this time. Too long. She was stretched thin with waiting, and for every day he was away, she floated farther from the shore.

Derek was the man who named her.

"You the ocean," he said. "That's what you are. You the ocean."

She believed him. And she believed, too, that he was the wall of rock that caught and held her rushing waters. She could swirl and rise in the crook of his body without fear. He grounded her with the weight of his chin on her head and the bend of his elbow around her middle as they slept. When he was around.

But Derek was in Chicago now. Or New Orleans. San Francisco, maybe. Wherever the sound of music had taken him this time. He left like he always did. With a kiss. A shrug of his shoulders.

"I'll call you," he said.

"When?" she asked.

"I'll call you," he'd repeated and then disappeared down the stairs and around the third-floor banister with his guitar.

For the first few days she enjoyed waiting. She took long baths with sweet salts after work. She washed her clothes (and the few shirts Derek left), perfumed the bed sheets, and hung fresh roses to dry over the doors and windows. She listened to bluesy jazz by candlelight, and lived those few days as if every moment held within it the possibility of his return. He didn't come. But he did call.

She didn't ask where he was, only when he was coming home.

"Soon as I can, baby. We have another couple stops to make before we head back that way."

"Who's we?" She wanted to ask, but didn't.

"What're you wearing?" he whispered.

It was late. She didn't want to tell him, but she did.

"My blue nightie," she whispered back.

"Mmmm."

* * *

After two weeks, he still had not returned. One by one, the rose petals fell to the floor, dried, and became dust beneath her feet. At night, she slept with the windows open and listened for the sound of his guitar to drift up from the street four stories down. The wind that rushed in through the open windows turned the bathwater cold. It shook the bed and made her dream she was drowning. She cradled the phone in her sleep. She dragged it into the bathroom while she showered. And when she had to run to the store for coffee or chocolate or cigarettes, she took the receiver off the hook so that if Derek called, he would get a busy signal and try back a few minutes later.

He had left before. Never for this long, but she still believed he was coming back. While she waited, she sat in the dry dust of rose petals and embroidered the sleeves of her dresses with pink and red butterflies. She decorated the pockets of her jeans with deep-sea fish, the cuffs of her shirts with leaves like ivy. While she sewed, she turned the radio up loud to distract herself from the wind that flooded her ears with the sound of water. It could have been hours or days that she sat this way; her hands busy, refusing to wait in stillness like the rest of her body.

After some time, even her art became impatient. The wings of the butterflies began to beat against each other, the deep-sea fish began to jump, and the leaves like ivy threatened to grow up her arms and around her neck and bind her to the spot if she refused to move. Then the phone rang, and she did not answer it. Instead, she let it ring while she pulled herself up from the dust, slipped into her high heels, painted her eyelids with glitter, and stepped out to meet the evening. The phone was still ringing when she shut the door behind her.

* * *

The music dropped heavy and loud in the dark room. Shadowy bodies channeled the rhythm and moved together like the flames of a fire. In corners, sisters in shiny lipstick stood against the walls and arched the smalls of their backs to meet the bodies of men who moved in close enough to smell them. At the bar, brothers leaned back on elbows, sipped drinks and surveyed the scene with untelling eyes.

She did not stop at the bar on her way to the dance floor. She did not look to see whom she might recognize or who might recognize her. She went straight for the speaker and stood before it with her eyes closed until the music filled her and sought release through her limbs.

Movement was all she wanted. She found it and was satisfied. Until she felt a pair of strong, soft hands on her hips. The heat of the hands guided her through the music and stirred the longing that sat weighty beneath her breastbone. She smiled sadly with her back to him and let him pull her close. When he did, she could smell him. He smelled of cool earth and something sweet and salty that she couldn't place but which reminded her of herself. It was some time before she turned around to look at him. In this darkness, with the swell of music around them, his crooked, too-cool smile made her want to forget everything she ever knew and start all over. Start fresh. It was a dangerous, thrilling thing, to want, at this very moment, what she knew she could have.

"I promise to be nice," she wanted to say. But she said nothing.

Instead she drifted back into the rhythm, to the heat of his hands on her hips, the scent of him that she couldn't quite place. For what could've been hours, or only minutes, they sweated in the safety of this shadowy crowd, in the driving pulse of the music. Then, while the lights were still low and the atmosphere was still heavy with seduction, she followed him to the bar and gave him her number. He kissed her on the cheek before she left. She didn't expect him to follow her out, and he didn't. But she did mean it when she said he could call.

"Anytime," she said. And she meant that, too.

*   *   *

The sweet-salty of him was strong, even beneath the layers of club-smoke on her clothes. She climbed weary into bed with the dust of rose petals clinging to the bottoms of her feet. She hummed herself to sleep and wondered why she recognized his scent when she had never seen his face before. What was it? And why did it remind her of herself?

This time, when the phone rang, she answered it. She had been dreaming something still, like winter trees or solid earth, and it took her a few minutes to know who was calling. They were in the middle of a conversation before she was fully awake.

"I was hoping you'd say that, baby," he said. It was then that she realized it was not Derek on the phone, but was instead the brother with the hot hands and the crooked smile from the club. At that same instant, she smelled him on her skin, the sweet-salty pulling her into full consciousness.

"And why is that?" she asked drowsily, playing along, rather than giving away that she had only just now entered the conversation.

"Because there are a couple of things I'd like to show you, too."

The wind brushed through the windows and the curtains danced lazily.

The moonlight shone blue in the room.

It wasn't supposed to be a game. But after such a long, tiring wait, it felt good knowing she could have this if she really wanted it. Knowing that if she held out her hand, he would eat from it. And even if Love walked out on her with a guitar on his back, she could find a way to forget. At least for a short time.

So she played what he wanted her to play. He teased her and she teased him back. While they engaged this way, she recalled the too-cool of his crooked smile. The sound of his voice drew upon her longing and made her hungry.

"Do you want to fuck me?" she asked, knowing full well that he did. It was in his answer that she finally found the source of his scent.

"I would love to make love to you."

The source was more a who, than a what. She saw the girl clear as spring water. The one who held his hand and shared his bed. The one whose forehead was still wet with his kiss.

She should have stopped then. She should have said goodnight and hung up. She was not interested in boys with ex-girlfriends on their breath. But it was this tenderness beneath the surface of his game that she wanted for herself. The hunger was now beyond her control.

She felt suddenly like a big fish. A big hungry fish with teeth strong enough to crunch through bone all the way down to the soft-soft of marrow. It would be so tasty, so perfect and delicious on her big fish tongue. She should have stopped then, but she couldn't. An enormous wave surged up in her, pushed against her belly from the inside, and sent her reeling. She was light-headed, and with nothing else to hold onto, she reached for the swelling. She dipped the fingers of one hand into the river and held the phone in the other. Though she never meant to play an unfair game, by the time he said he was coming over, it was too late. She already came. Quietly, she came.

Then it was over. For her it was. In that one tiny instant, the possibility of him dissolved, and he became nothing more than a little fish with no bone to crunch at all. No marrow to suck. Just a little fish, sad and lonely, with not even enough muscle to retrieve the wet of his kiss from the forehead of one girl, and certainly not enough to hold back the rushing waters of another.

She slept well that night, interrupted by nothing. No image, no sound. No dreams. It was a deep, still-water rest. In the morning, the sun breathed light into the room. A breeze fluttered through the curtains and scattered the dust of dry roses. She spent the morning in peaceful silence, waiting patiently for the strum of a roving guitar.

Chapter Three
Cats & Tambourines

My man got no sleep that night. "Did she just play me? Or did I play myself?" were the echoes running across his skin every time sleep started to flirt with him. Frustrated with the night, he got out of the bed at about five thirty to check the one thing that gave him love every morning: the sunrise.

Mr. Hancock, the only black man in the neighborhood with a bodega, was making his way across the street to open shop. With slivers of sunlight sliding between the buildings making the horizon, Dante wondered *what if*.

What if I rolled over to her crib anyway? Her fiancé? How she gonna have a fiancé and be on the phone with a brother like me? Kickin' it like we been backstroking together for years. Shit. Even if she really does have a fiancé, so what? That there river came from *my* breath. Not his.

I should have rolled over there and told her: "That right there is Dante's river, sugar. Now, you gonna let me christen the crest of this wave proper? Or are you gonna pass the time by lining up cats like me to get you off over the phone?"

Nah. I did the right thing by taking my ass home. If a sister ain't feeling me enough to say, "Come and bring it!" then I just need to stay here and keep it. With that, Dante took his tired, no-sleep-having behind back to bed, thanking God it was Saturday so he could get some rest for real.

The phone rang about eleven thirty, breaking up some dream about kissing Sadé. She was telling him that after the tamarind taste of his lips, she was gonna come out of her self-imposed exile to make music completely dedicated to him. The sharp sting of the ringer dissolved the picture before he could work out more details. Too lazy to get up and pick up the receiver, he just lay there and waited for the machine to answer.

"Too blessed for the best, too hot for Hell …. Yeah, yeah, you've just reached Dante. Tell me something love and I'll holla back." Jesus, I have got to change that trife ass message, he thought before the tone sounded.

"Hello, Dante. I know your behind is there. You need to pick up the phone. You better not be laying up with that skinny chick with the big tatas you was dancing with at the club last night. We only been broke up three days, mister. Damn. You could let a sister's juice dry off your lips before you go stepping into some other sister's house. Anyway, I need to talk to you, so get back with me."

Sheron, his ex.

Contemplating whether he should return her call now or a little later, he noticed there was a Siamese cat looking through his window from the fire escape. This puzzled him. Siamese cats didn't usually run stray in the city, and he knew Mrs. Jefferson didn't allow any kind of thing that wasn't human up in her apartment building.

Dante and the cat grilled each other for a long second before he figured out maybe "she" was hungry. "I barely got bone in the fridge though," he thought as he crept out of bed to search for something.

Scanning the barrens of his fridge, the only thing he spotted was some fresh broccoli and a carton of soymilk. "Well, miss, I hope you're a vegan," he laughed to himself while filling a saucer with some milk and making his lazy way back to the bedroom.

The phone rang again. But this time the voice was different. Familiar, though he couldn't place it.

"Hello? Hello? Dante, this is ... well, that's on you. I got something for you. I just hope your machine doesn't cut me off."

Intrigued and afraid to pick up the phone before she finished, he still couldn't place the butter-silk in her voice.

She continued. "'To watch him was like pouring wood root tonic on the back of my instincts. I got shook by the breeze fire in his walk. And when the smoke cleared, all I saw was handclaps scratching the back of my deepest fantasy. I could see us tasting tangerine tears that danced on our cheeks like Prince shaking tambourines.' Yeah, baby. That's for you ... from me."
Beep.

31

What the—? Who was that? He ran from the kitchen and rushed the phone to star 69 her before anyone else called. As the phone rang on the other end, he noticed that the cat was no longer at the window. "I guess I didn't move fast enough for you. Just like a sister."

His breath stopped short when the ringing stopped. In a split second that seemed like a week, he tried to figure out a plan. A word, a sentence, something ... only to be greeted by an automated voice.

"I'm sorry. This number cannot be reached by this method."

Shook by what seemed to be a lasting trend of bizarre encounters with the opposite sex, Dante reluctantly moved on with his Saturday. First, he sipped the milk from the saucer, then he placed it in the sink, turned on Sadé, and stepped in the shower.

For some reason, the mystery call left him feeling energized and he decided that he was going to make this Saturday a good day. After the shower, he put on his black-on-black Adidas, some khakis and a gray tank top. After placing sandalwood oil in all the proper places, he went downstairs to Mr. Hancock's spot and bought some fruit. Then started to make his way to the park, daydreaming of sisters, cats, and tambourines.

Chapter Four
Treasure the Savior

"I don't give a fuck who you are or how much money you gon' spend on me, just leave me alone!"

The woman's words ricocheted down the block bouncing off buildings and into Dante's ears. A loud squawk burst from behind him. He twisted his head back just quick enough to glimpse the curled claws of a flock of fleeing birds. His eyes lifted with the black flapping wings, then the street was empty. Dante turned back to the woman. She stood near the corner; hands on hips, face contorted in anger. A man materialized from the shadows of a deserted building. Dante's protection reflex unfurled as the man prowled up to the woman's side, predatory, hungry. Dante's eyes flew to the couple's hands. There were no broken bottles clutched in fists, no guns resting in palms. He felt something like safety slip through his spine. He averted his gaze and approached the corner.

He was now close enough to smell ill intent on the man's breath.

"You ain't gotta be that way," the man mumbled, his chin jutting out, nose twitching like a hunter full of the scent of his prey. Dante looked away. He couldn't stand staring naked aggression dead in the face. The woman whipped her head around and caught Dante mid-stride.

"There you are," she said, brushing over Dante's face with quick eyes. He paused. She leaned towards him. "Why you take so long?"

Dante fixed his mouth to ask her if she was crazy, but was stopped by the flash of a hard plea in her gray eyes. He shrugged his shoulders instead.

"I don't wanna hear no excuses," she said wagging a finger at him.

"What? This your man or something?" the man broke in, arms spread in confrontation.

The woman sucked her teeth and turned her back to him. The tightness of her face betrayed her anxiety. Dante felt her desperation leap onto his shoulders and cling to his neck. The man's presence swirled around them like a sudden gust of wind, violent and forceful.

"Let's go," Dante finally said. Those two words melted the hardness in the woman's face. The tension dispersed. His threat deflated, the man pushed his hands into his pockets and slipped back into darkness.

The woman's fingers encircled Dante's wrist and led him away. As they turned the corner, he glanced over his shoulder and caught the glimmer of cat eyes blinking in the shadows. He slipped two tangerines into his pocket. He kept one in his hand, rolling it around his palm with his fingers. The woman walked in silence; head fixed forward, neck held stiff. He stuck his thumb into the tangerine and pried the peel from the fruit. As he separated the fruit into sections, the woman looked back over her shoulder. She saw sunlight, an empty corner, no sign of her harasser. She let out a relieved gust of air.

As bits of tangerine burst across his tongue, Dante felt her hand lightly lodge into the crook of his elbow. He glanced at her profile, then turned away. His eyes swept over the glinting windshields of parked cars. Above him, the dark silhouettes of birds dove arcs and circles overhead. Leaves tumbled across the sidewalk, pushed along by an eager breeze. Dante exhaled noisily prompting the woman to speak.

"So, what's your name, o' savior of mine?"

"Dante," he said and spit out a tangerine seed.

"Oh, thank you Dante, I will dance at your wedding. Do you have one planned? I can tap, and salsa, and do African dance."

He glanced at her, certain she was kidding, but her face didn't hold one hint of a joke. His eyes wandered down her body. He scanned the layers of muslin wrapped around her breasts and torso. He paused briefly at the curve of her hips, noting the tight communion of cloth and flesh. A long pea-green skirt hugged her waist and swept out, hovering just over her ankles. Each step revealed sturdy feet covered in sandals that seemed to be made of duct tape. He heard the jangle of bracelets as her free hand lifted and offered itself to him. Dante clasped her hand and shook it. The bangles danced from her wrist to her forearm.

"My name is Treelawn. Don't say nothin' about my name. My parents fucked me over with it, but at least they were being creative."

After a pause she asked, "You gon' share?"

"I got one just for you, Tree," Dante said and pulled a tangerine out of his pocket.

"It's not Tree, it's Treelawn. Though Tree does sound kind of deep. Mind if I use it?" Treelawn was abruptly silent as she squeezed the fruit with long fingers, then lifted it to her nose to check the scent. "What are you doing around here? I never saw you before. What kind of work do you do? You look kind of corporate, but then again you don't. Hmmm, maybe you work in a cafe or maybe you're a bike messenger or something. You're probably a frustrated artist. You can call me Treasure, that's nicer, right?"

"I guess."

"You don't talk much."

"Forgive me for saying so, but you talk too much."

"You got good manners," Treasure shot back and removed her arm from around Dante's.

He shrugged his shoulders and pulled the last tangerine from his pocket. They walked in silence feeling the wind push at their backs. When they reached the next corner Dante stopped.

"Who was that guy?" he asked motioning behind him.

"What? Back there on the corner?"

Dante nodded and popped half the tangerine into his mouth.

"Oh, just one of the daily details that make a woman's life hell." Dante's cheeks swelled with sweet citric acid as Treasure ran across the street and leapt to touch an overhanging tree branch. She grabbed a bunch of leaves, ripped them from the tree, and brought them to her chest. After making sure the street was clear, Dante sauntered after her.

"So you don't know him?"

"Nah," Treasure said while walking backwards. "He's just one of a million assholes who think he got rights to any woman he think is cute."

She spread her fingers and watched the leaves float from her palm and scatter onto the concrete.

"Aww, stop it, women got it easy. Somebody always tryin' to tell them they cute."

"And what's so nice about that?"

Dante shook his head. "You crazy? I know girls like it."

"How do you know? Ask yo' mama. Ask yo' sister. Ask your girlfriend what it's like to have every piece of your body up for discussion every hour of the day."

"You mean you don't like gettin' compliments?"

Treasure paused as she peeled her tangerine and thought about his question.

"There's a difference between getting a compliment and a demand, or a compliment and an intrusion. When, 'Can I have your number?' is attached, it ain't a compliment, it's manipulation."

"So you don't want no man to appreciate your beauty?"

"Yeah, over dinner, during a conversation, at work, not yelled at me from the corner twenty million times a day."

"You're a little arrogant."

"Arrogant my ass. I'm a realist." She paused to place a tangerine section into her mouth. "Man, this tangerine is sweet!" She held up her hands as if testifying and leaned back while the fruit's juices leapt from taste bud to taste bud. "Mmm!" she grunted in approval. "Listen, have you ever watched these men? If you stand on the corner and watch them, you'll see. It ain't about me. They'll talk to damn near every woman that passes. All you need is a nice round female ass and they're gonna talk to you. It's like some kind of hormonal reaction. They can't just admire your ass from afar. They got to tell you that you have a nice ass, ask you how it smells, and tell you what they would like to do with it. Now what kind of a compliment is that?"

Treasure swallowed and Dante laughed.

"They see a sexy lady passing, they want to let her know they think she's fine, what do you want them to do?"

"You think a woman can't see your appreciation in your eyes? If you just smile at her. Or say good morning. Believe me, she'll get it, and feel good about it." Treasure's arms flew up as if to get into the conversation. Her jerking head spoke volumes. "But nooooooooo, they don't just want to speak, they want to demand a conversation while you walkin' down the street minding your business. Shit, I could be late or I could be composing a poem in my head and they just—"

"You're a poet?"

"Yeah."

"Read me one."

"Not on the first date."

Dante chuckled.

"So where we going?" Treasure asked.

"We?"

"Yeah, I'm hungry. Let's have lunch."

Dante shot her a suspicious glance, and Treasure caught the dirty thought contained within. "The conversation was cute," it said, "but you ain't about to con me for a meal."

"Oh don't get all anal," she said and held up a twenty-dollar bill. "My treat."

Dante's eyes shot from the money to Treasure's face. He felt something tight and mistrustful uncoil inside him. He fixed his mouth to refuse Treasure's offer, but when he looked into her face she nodded her head as if to say, "You know you want to." Laughter slipped from his lips and dissolved his reluctance.

"All right, bet, but let's pick up something and eat in the park."

"And stain my fine linen?" Treasure joked brushing her palms over her skirt.

"Is that a yes?"

"Yes, Mr. Dante. Yes, yes, yes!"

* * *

Treasure leaned back and sighed. Empty take-out cartons littered the grass around her. Dante shook his head in amusement. She had laughed at him when he ordered tofu at the deli. She called it vegetable Spam and ordered grilled chicken instead. Yet a few seconds after she finished her chicken, she asked him if he was done with the tofu. Before the, "Yes," was fully out of his mouth, she grabbed the carton. She left the forks in their wrappers preferring to lift tofu chunks to her lips with her fingers. She finished her meal by licking her hands and lips clean.

"We shoulda got some bread," she said, sitting up suddenly. Behind her, the sun glistened off the man-made lake where a group of kids were pretend fishing. To her right, the thick trunk of a tree stood strong and solid.

Dante rolled his eyes. "I can't believe you're still thinking about food."

She shrugged her shoulders impishly.

"Look. Look at all the empty containers you got around you. Looks like a deli graveyard, and you're still hungry!"

She laughed and lay down on her side. He stretched his legs out in front of him and leaned back on his elbows.

"I like food," she said, and rolled onto her back with her arms behind her head.

"That's an understatement," he said. He stood up, stretched lazily, then wandered over to the tree.

"What do you like?" Treasure asked in a lazy sleepy drawl.

"Jamaica," he replied and pulled hard green pellets from the tree's branches.

"What?"

"Jamaica. The beach, the fried fish and bammy, the mountains. The landscape, the entire island is amazing." He paused and pitched the pellets toward the lake, one by one.

"That's cool, but I meant what do you like to do?"

"That is what I like to do, I like to go to Jamaica."

"I never been."

Dante squatted on his haunches and said wistfully, "You haven't lived until you've dove off a cliff in Negril and swam naked in the ocean."

"I must be dead then," Treasure remarked and closed her eyes.

"And what a lovely corpse you are."

Her eyes popped open and she sucked her teeth in irritation. "Ohhh, don't start that crap."

"What crap?"

"The you're-so-beautiful crap."

"You're a weirdo."

"No I'm not, I'm an angel."

"An angel of what?"

She sat up and leaned towards him. "That's for me to know and you to find out."

"Who's starting now?"

Treasure turned her head away from Dante sharply.

"You hear that?" she asked.

He cocked his head and squinted his eyes. He didn't hear anything.

"No."

She jumped to her feet and pulled at his arm. "Stand up, let's go look."

He stood and surveyed the trash lying on the ground. "We can't leave all this shit here."

"Come on, we'll be right back."

Dante crossed his arms and shot her a look.

"All right, damn!" She scooped the empty cartons into the plastic take-out bag. She stomped over to the trashcan and dropped the bag in with a flourish. She returned to Dante's side with her hand on her hip.

"Happy now, Mr. Clean?"

He started to say something sarcastic, but instead bit his lip in what he hoped was an offhand, sexy move. He pinched her cheek.

"Yeah, actually, I am."

"Well, let's go."

Treasure led the way over a hill to a courtyard in the middle of the park. Dante looked around and shook his head.

"There's nothing here, Treasure."

"Oh, yes there is."

"Well, I don't see anything."

"Let's sit on the bench."

The light pleasure that had settled in after lunch quickly fled Dante's body. His shoulders slouched under the weight of suspicion. He wondered what game she was playing, wondered if he could figure out the rules. She sat down and waited for Dante to join her. She stretched her legs out, put her hands behind her head, and pretended to relax. Dripping with reluctance, Dante stepped towards the bench. He slowly eased his body down next to hers.

"Let's talk about our fears," she said suddenly.

"Our what?"

"The shit we're scared of, you know, our fears."

"Where the fuck did that come from?" He leaned forward, fighting the sudden desire to run.

"I'm afraid of the currents in the ocean," she said while staring off into the trees that lined the edge of the park. As she spoke, a fat, dirty, white dog wandered into the courtyard and plopped down on the concrete. "I jump in when it's calm, but then the current grabs me and drags me further out. I turn the other way, but I can't get nowhere. I'm swimming real hard and I feel like I ain't moving, that scares the shit out of me. I feel like I'm never going to get the fuck out."

She paused and looked at him expectantly. He said nothing.

"I'm afraid of intimacy." Another dog—mangy, skinny, and black—wandered into the courtyard. Dante's head shot up. He speared Treasure with a look of discomfort, but she kept talking. "There's been a couple of people who got to me. I know it's supposed to be a good thing, but getting open screws with my head. I get with somebody I really dig and I freeze up. I know if I lose control, I'll lose myself. And I ain't about to give nothin' up. Not for nothin'. Not for nobody. Love is fucked up. I dodge that shit like it's fatal. In the end, I just bounce between beds and hearts. It's fucked up but it keeps me safe."

Dante crossed his arms. A searing heat exploded in his gut. He couldn't figure out what Treasure was up to, but her words were beginning to spook him. She had picked two of his fears right out of the air. Not only were they his fears, but the words she used were his words. She was stealing his thoughts, thoughts he hadn't even voiced to himself. He flexed his fingers and grasped his sides. His muscles strained as he held on to his body. Still, he said nothing.

"I'm afraid of getting someone pregnant. I'm afraid of revenge for my sins. I'm afraid I fucked over my one true chance at love. I'm afraid love was never meant for me."

He began to twitch. He tried to shrug off his discomfort, but her words lodged in his throat. He coughed, heaving big dry breaths from his chest. The fat, dirty, white dog bared its teeth and began to whine. The noise crawled under Dante's skin and trampled on his nerves. He jumped to his feet. He took a step and coughed, stepped, and coughed again. He stopped in front of Treasure and leaned close to her face.

"Who are you?" he whispered.

She ignored his question. With her eyes firmly fixed on his, she kept voicing his fears. Dante began pacing. Both dogs were barking now. He clasped his hands over his ears to block out the sound.

"Get out of my head, get out of my head, get out of my head."

He mumbled the command like a mantra as if his words could shut Treasure up. She jumped up from her seat and pulled his hands from his ears.

"What are you so afraid of?" she yelled. "What has you shook?"

Dante growled and stalked away. He was stopped by a small caramel-colored dog sitting in his path. He wanted to walk around her, but the minute he looked into her sorrowful eyes, he was frozen in place. It was as if he was staring into those round brown eyes for an eternity. When Dante finally blinked, the air started sucking height and weight from his body. He looked up and saw himself: head fixed downwards, arms frozen at his sides. He looked down and found he had four brown paws instead of hands and feet. He opened his mouth to scream, but could only yelp.

He blinked again and again as if that motion could return him to his body. The snarling dogs made him tremble. Somehow he knew: they wanted his dog flesh. It was teeth he felt first, as the skinny black dog began the assault. Dante whimpered as the incisors flew past his fur and pierced his skin. He shook the dog off before blood bubbled to the surface, but he couldn't run. He tried to move his human body, struggled to lift an arm, a leg, anything to help himself, but his limbs were dead weight and would not be moved. He felt claws next, as the fat white dog jumped on his back. This time the skin did rip, tearing flesh, exposing muscle. Dante threw desperate kicks with his brown paws. He dipped his dog head trying to avoid the assault. A whisper from Treasure's direction caused hysteria to riot through Dante's body. "You can't escape," her voice said. "You can't."

Snapping teeth, biting, splitting skin. Dante's stomach felt on fire. His tiny dog body began to crumble under the onslaught. The pain was beginning to choke him. He felt his will to survive slipping from his wounds. A horrible sound ripped from his gut, full and hoarse. Moments passed before he realized his anguish had emerged as a scream, not a bark or a yelp. He wanted to touch himself, check his body with his hands, but he could not move. He stood stiff in his body, releasing ragged, relieved breaths. The two dogs' teeth were bloody now. The little brown dog lay unconscious, completely exposed to canine viciousness. Dante's chest swelled. He found paralysis worse than being pounced upon. Yet a terror gripped him when the dogs turned away from their conquered prey. They fixed bloodthirsty eyes on him. A low snarl announced their approach. As their claws and jaws neared him, his mind went blank. Every mental impulse dissolved. It was as if a white sheet unfurled in his mind. All breath, thought, feeling was stilled. He was a gasp, a choke, anything held and anxious and still.

Suddenly Treasure was there. Her arms scooping up the little caramel-colored dog. She was calm as the black dog leapt, teeth bared, to re-attack the little dog. The black jaws closed around her forearm, then separated as if shocked. The dog fell to the ground, a puddle of whimpering impotence. What had Treasure done to cause it to lose strength and lay in shuddering surrender? The white dog snarled, but Treasure didn't bother to look in its direction. Under her stare, the black dog shrank down to nothing, then disappeared. Alone now, the white dog growled and ripped into Treasure's calf. Treasure glared, Dante watched, as it stupidly repeated the black dog's fate.

When she had disappeared the white dog, Treasure grasped Dante's shoulder. He didn't move. She squeezed until she felt bone. Then his eyelids moved. Blink, blink, blink. Treasure shook him as hard as she could. He took a slow step backward and raised his hands to his face. They were shaking from wrists to fingertips. He touched his chest, his hips, his knees, his feet. He looked around him. The courtyard was empty.

Treasure reached for his hand, but he moved away. She had morphed from a cute, quirky woman into something dangerous and frightful. She grabbed for his hand again. This time their fingers touched. When her skin met his, peace swept through his body. His racing heart slowed to a calm, steady beat. She led him back to the park bench and gently pushed him against the wood. His head fell back as he dropped into a sitting position. Gulping breaths shook every muscle in his body. He mumbled to himself, trying to regain equilibrium. He avoided looking at the little brown dog, even as it peeked at him from the cradle of Treasure's arms. She grasped the dog under its belly and held it out with both hands.

"Take her," she said.

Fear paraded across Dante's face. He refused to touch the animal. She tucked the dog under her arm and pressed her palm to Dante's throat.

"Your fears will rule you if you do not speak them," she whispered.

A moan erupted from deep inside him. Her hand vibrated as his vocal cords quivered.

"Speak, Dante, speak."

He turned his face away as tears slid from beneath his eyelids. Treasure tightened her mouth in irritation and dropped the little dog onto his lap. She crossed her arms and waited. His lips refused to part in speech. She shook her head and walked away. Dante opened his mouth to call her back, but no sound came out. He could not speak. He could not stop her. He could only watch as she strode toward a seed of light. The seed swirled and unfurled into a shimmering curtain. Without looking back, she stepped into the curtain of light and disappeared. Dante fell back against the bench and placed a sweaty hand on his forehead. The dog looked up at him, Dante looked out at the empty earth, eyes lingering over the space where Treasure was swallowed by light.

Dante gasped for breath as if he were drowning. His head tossed from side to side as sleep retreated from his body. His eyes opened.

At first he saw nothing. Just the blackness of his dark apartment but he could hear the whisper of car tires in the distance. He propped himself up on his elbows and groaned. Looking around him, he saw his books. His television stared at him blankly, mutely. His computer's screensaver flashed the time, "3:01 AM". He fell back against his bed as his eyes roamed the ceiling in wonder. His head was thick with memory; his body ached for no good reason. A slight recollection of the dream world breezed over his skin. He squeezed his eyes shut and focused. Attempted to coax the dream into his consciousness, but it wouldn't be seduced. With his head still hazy, he rolled over, hoping to return to sleep.

Just as he was slipping back into unconsciousness, the contents of the dream invaded his mind. Treasure. The dogs. Him trapped in his own body. He saw the little dog sheltered in Treasure's arms. He remembered her touch, how she brought him back from terror.

"She saved me," he mumbled to himself.

"Ahhhh, Dante," he heard her voice whisper, "I haven't saved you yet."

He sat up quickly and looked around him. He was alone in his apartment. He lifted the sheets. Except for a few stray pillows, the bed was empty. He hung his upper body off the side of his bed and peeked underneath. Dark mounds of dirty clothes, magazines and DVDs lurked beneath his bed, but no Treasure. He shook his head. "I'm too young to be losing my mind," he thought.

He settled back against the pillows and touched himself. With every stroke, he evoked a facsimile of his most recent ex-girlfriend in his mind. He reassembled her curves, her scent, her sweetness to crowd the nightmare out of his consciousness. Soon he was slipping into orgasm, and just as suddenly into sleep. He settled his weight into the mattress and cuddled his ex-girlfriend in his imagination. As his fingers lazily remembered contours and crevices, the ghosts of the banished dogs prowled through his apartment. Beyond the cloak of Dante's sleep, the dogs barked chaos onto his walls and pissed territorially. As Dante dreamed of removing nylon fabric from female flesh, the dogs were roaming the length of his apartment. As he was penetrating a phantom, they were curling contentedly on the floor, claiming the corners of his home as their own.

Chapter Five
Wet Dreams

D ante woke up in a sweat so cold he shivered. The bed
sheets beneath him were completely soaked, as if
they'd been used to mop up a spill. And he'd sweat so
much that his cum hadn't had a chance to dry, so it sat slick and
sticky between his legs like chicken grease between the fingers
of a child.

Since he first met Treasure over a year ago, Dante
discovered that every time he slept with her, he dreamt about
the day they met and being attacked by stray dogs.

He thought back, retracing his steps. He'd left the
apartment, bought some fruit from Mr. Hancock and started

walking to the park ... but he'd forgotten his cell phone and come back home for it. Treasure had been waiting at his front door, looking lovely, and he never made it back outside.

When he reached out for her he realized he was alone. Treasure had literally come and gone, leaving nothing behind but her panties, her idiosyncratic calling card, as if to let him know she'd been there and they'd fucked, as if her panties weren't good enough to put back on and take home once she let a man slide them from around her waist.

Dante really didn't mind a woman leaving them at his house, his problem with Treasure was that she hid hers and if he didn't find them they'd resurface like land mines and always at the wrong damn time, particularly when another woman was spending the night.

The city lights flooded through the blades of his open blinds, illuminating the bedroom. They were bright enough that he didn't need a lamp and he only had to turn the overhead light on when he decided to write. Dante tossed his legs out from under the sheets, sat up on the edge of his bed and peered at his alarm clock. It was one thirty in the morning; he'd slept the entire evening away. And all he could remember was going out to buy milk and returning home to find Treasure sitting at his door. His first reaction was to firmly ask her to leave, especially after the whole Eva thing, but when he noticed the short African print skirt she was wearing—the one that stopped seductively at mid-thigh—and the black leotard that barely held her breasts inside the straining fibers of their threads, he got weak. And all his urges about asking her to leave were completely suppressed.

The two of them barely even talked anymore; they just felt each other up and had sex. He must have fallen asleep shortly thereafter and was amazed that he'd slept so long.

Dante lit a half-used spliff lying in the ashtray on the nightstand next to his bed and began his search. He ripped the sheets and pillows off his bed, lifted his mattress and peered under it. He searched the floor of his closet, the pockets of his clothes and behind the dresser drawer of his room. He walked slowly through his living room, pulling up the cushion of his futon and feeling behind the books on his bookshelf, yet still he found no signs. He ransacked his apartment like a spiteful burglar who wanted to let his victims know that he had been there. Luckily, he only lived in a two-room apartment, but in his search he still came up empty handed.

"I give up," he sighed. "She always finds some new place to hide her shit," Dante mumbled to himself.

He threw his hands up in surrender and retired to his kitchen for a drink. He pulled on his refrigerator door and frowned in disgust. He'd found Treasure's panties stuffed in the mouth of his brand new carton of milk.

"Ain't this about a bitch," he grumbled, pulling them free. He cupped them to his nose and sniffed the sweet, slightly pungent smell of female arousal that sat in its crotch like an invisible lining. Scents were a fetish of his. So were one-night stands, but in his flawed approach to all matters concerning the heart he'd tried to turn each one into a relationship. He leaned back against his refrigerator and remembered how he'd tried to do that with Treasure. The only problem was that he had been involved with Sheron at the time and instead of ending either relationship, he became romantically involved with them both. That was until Sheron found one of Treasure's calling cards balled up in the corner of his closet. He hadn't even known leaving her panties behind was a habit of hers until Sheron screamed on him while clutching it in her hand. He always found out shit the hard way. But after that he conducted a sweep and found she'd left several more pairs balled up and hidden like old rat poison throughout his apartment.

But he'd found those a few days later—after he'd gotten his sight back, because Sheron had blinded him temporarily when she pepper-sprayed him with the mini canister she kept on her key chain. Afterwards, she was so guilt ridden that she stayed with him until he regained his sight, but his cheating and her retaliatory assault marked the beginning of their end. They became both the combatants and casualties of an emotionally violent relationship that took one year to finally kill itself.

Dante finished smoking his spliff and tossed the roach in the sink. The visions from his nightmarish attack by the recurring stray dogs of his dream began haunting him again. He'd been free of his recurring nightmare for months, but having sex with women he wasn't supposed to was one of the many triggers that conjured it up. Sheron was the one person who could soothe him after his anxiously violent dreams. But when they broke up a few days ago, he vowed he'd never speak to her again. That left only one other person he felt comfortable enough to call.

* * *

The club was always packed on Saturday nights. And Sheron could clear at least five hundred dollars in twenty-minute's time whenever she performed her illicitly famous shower scene. It was so popular that she'd developed a cult following for it. And like with all good cults, her worshippers came to pay homage to their god.

Sheron stepped into the glass cage positioned above backstage and looked around. It reminded her of the man-sized test tubes in movies where scientists placed aliens on display to be examined.

When she gave the technician the nod, her glass cage was lowered by a small crane onto the center of the L-shaped stage that sat in the heart of the club.

The stage was surrounded by tables with four chairs each and cushioned lounge chairs lined the mirrored club walls with tiny coffee tables in between. Pussykatz seated about one hundred fifty men and was usually filled to capacity but on Saturday nights it swelled to about three hundred. This was her money night, the night when table dances sold like pussy in prison and drinks from the bar sold like life jackets on a sinking cruise ship.

Sheron wore a see-through raincoat and beneath it, a red thong. The muscles in her long, taut, dark brown legs flexed when she began to move and her calf muscles were given added definition from being buttressed by her bright red pumps.

Water sprayed down lightly from a retractable showerhead extending from the ceiling and she began her dance. She ripped open her raincoat and let it slide down her arms to the shower floor. The spotlight hit her and lit her up like a world famous diva at a sold out concert. Sheron unhooked her detachable thong at the waist and tossed it to the side. Then she took a bar of soap from the built-in soap dish and bathed. She caressed herself in circular motions until she was completely lathered, intently rubbing the spots on her body that drew the best reactions from the crowd. The water from the shower began to spray harder gradually, until the last of the soap was completely rinsed from her body. She stepped out of the glass cage, dripping wet. Beads of water covered her skin and sparkled like the glitter on a sequined gown as she walked down the stage like a runway model strutting down a catwalk. Once she made it to the edge of the stage she turned her back to her feverously aroused audience, dramatically parted her legs, and leaned over until the top of her head touched the stage floor. The howl of the audience rushed through her like an injected drug.

Ones, fives and ten dollar bills pelted her onstage like raindrops from a sudden downpour and she felt the excitement of the crowd swirl around her like wind. She was in her element and while onstage she controlled the weather. She could make it rain money better than any other dancer in the club. And to flaunt her power over the sky Sheron rolled over into a partial somersault and stood poised on her head. She spread her legs until they leveled parallel with the stage floor and gave the men who came to the edge of the stage an eyeful of what they wanted most. The audience roared, the music blasted, and the bass from the speakers reverberated through her until it became indistinguishable from he very beat of her heart.

Money was literally being thrown at her now. Ones became fives, tens became twenties, and twenties became fifties. One of her parishioners came to the stage and planted a one hundred dollar bill into the open palm of her upraised third hand. It contracted and clutched the bill with the immediacy of a steel bear trap and more amazed men blessed her with the tithing of one hundred dollar bills just to see her do it again. They were her congregation. This strip club, her church. And the open hand between her legs was an offering plate that filled without end.

* * *

"Aint nothing to interpret, Dante, you're a dog and you don't like the man you're becoming as a result of it."

"But the dream was so real," Dante confessed. He was uneasy about being so revealing to Malik even though they were best friends, had been boys since grade school and knew each other better than they knew themselves. Still, Malik had an advanced degree in psychology and tended to analyze him in such accurate fashion that their telephone conversations always left Dante uncomfortable. But Malik and Sheron were the only ones he could ever turn to when his life seemed fit for hell, or whenever he woke up from the nightmare of the stray dogs that haunted him without remorse.

"And Treasure? Ain't that the sista you cheated on Sheron with?"

"Yeah, so?"

"Well, hell, there it is, man. Dream interpreted. Your dreams are easy 'cause they're always visited by the last woman you did wrong. Man, I oughta charge you for my time, 'cause I'm performing some groundbreakin' therapy on your ass tonight."

Dante hated Malik's arrogance, which seemed to flare up whenever he was right.

"Whatever, bruh. But, damn, why is it that every woman I sleep with pops up in my dreams, and why do those damn dogs get more and more vicious?"

"Maybe it's because you're becoming more and more vicious yourself. And maybe Treasure was in your dream this time because you're seeing yourself from the eyes of the last woman you fucked and left."

"Fuck you. She left me."

"Really? Then why are y'all still having sex?"

Dante always wanted to disagree with Malik when he felt he was being harshly judged, but he could never argue against Malik's logic so his only other alternative was truth.

"I'm scared of being intimate, dammit. Treasure and Sheron broke me down, okay? They made me second-guess myself and question my judgment about everything."

"But you cheated on them."

"I know. It's because I'm scared as hell of getting close to women because in the back of my mind I feel like they'll grow to not want me. I'm scared of being rejected."

"So you find their flaws and reject them, just like you did with Eva. Get rid of them before they can get rid of you, huh?"

"I know, I know, I'm fucked up."

"No, you're not. Your ass is just being melodramatic again. And you're simply letting one or two bad relationships ruin all your others."

"Well, maybe I just like having sex. You ever think about that?"

"Spoken like a true pimp ... but, you're not a pimp, Dante."

"Maybe."

"'Maybe.' That's all you've got to say?"

"Uh-huh."

"Well look, it's two twenty in the morning and I'ma get off this phone and go to bed, but just promise me one thing."

"What's that?"

"Whatever you do, don't call Sheron. Leave the sista alone. You two have hurt each other enough already as it is. Promise me, Dante. Hello …? Dante …?"

"A'ight man, damn. I promise."

* * *

Sheron carefully navigated her way down the stairs of the stage, each step made perilous by her six inch spiked heels.

"Girl, you fine as hell, come dance for me and my boys," one of her lust-drunk fans uttered as he grabbed her arm.

"I will, baby. Let Mama go dry off and change first," Sheron said as she skillfully slipped out of his clutch and gingerly fought through the swelling crowd and into the dancer's locker room located at the back of the club.

She dropped her raincoat and thong in a heap at her locker door and sat on the bench adjacent to it as she counted out fifteen hundred dollars in tips.

She heard her beeper going off inside her locker and opened it to see Dante's phone number on display. She immediately erased it, because at two twenty five in the morning he either wanted to talk about that damn recurring nightmare or he was making a booty call. She assumed the latter, because he hadn't had the former in a while, so she shut her pager off to help fight the urge to call him if he decided to page her again. She collected her costume into her travel bag, changed into her street clothes and slipped out the back door of the club.

How dare he make a booty call to me, she thought, as she walked toward the subway a block away. After not returning my phone call for days, this fool thinks he's gonna get some ass?

She became so wrapped up in her anger that she couldn't even remember walking down the subway stairs and through the turnstile. But as she stood there waiting for her train to come she pulled his poem from her purse one more time.

You were the only woman in the world that night
looking lost in your raincoat like a forgotten child left outside
in a storm
your thoughts were focused on your dance
as the greedy stares from flocks of vultures attempted to
devour you on stage

You left the stage and stood in a
darkened corner of the club
ignoring the celebration
of boisterous men beckoning for
your affection with handfuls
of ten dollar bills

I had come to burn my troubles away
to get high off of second-hand smoke
and numb the jagged edges of a broken heart
by briefly receiving the undivided
attentions of the
women who were paid, by the song, to give it

and with the deeply voiced speakers
belching bass lines and hooks

and the shadows in the
room hiding our faces like veils
it was so easy just to step into the shadows
and disappear in the dark

But you looked so alone that
I wanted you next to me
because even through the
shadows I could see
that we were twins

We didn't even
know each other's
names when I asked you
to dance
yet we walked into the
private room where lovers, under contract, go to be alone

we wrote poetry that night
our words spoken in touch and
written across the pages of
each other's faces
using our lips as pens, and
our tongues dipped in an erotic ink
we momentarily rewrote who we were
and lived solely for each other as
time softly ticked away
towards the end of the
last song
and when the lights came on I was changed

revived by the fleeting moments spent connected to you

I don't know what effect that night had on you
or if the flame of my memory stayed lit awhile
before being blown out by the next invisible man
but you saved me that night
you brought me back from the
emotionally dead
I left that room with a heartbeat
with a pulse and
with a new thirst to love the
next woman who'd one day
find her way to me

it was the best thirty minutes of my life
the best money I'd ever spent
and in the shadows where men go to
disappear, I chose to
reemerge
for thirty minutes in the dark, you were the
best friend I'd ever had

Every time she read his poem, she cried. He was her weakness, her one temptation, he owned her with his words because no man had ever written to her in such sincere and moving ways. And no man had ever been struck enough by her to make her the muse for a poem. She fell in love with him all over again each time she read his words, and she kept his poem neatly folded in her purse; its creases worn from being constantly opened and refolded. She had pulled it out at least once a day for the past two years and it was the last remaining hold he had over her … his way with words.

At first Dante was just another customer to her, one of the dozens of men with at least ten dollars to spend. And all she had to do was undress while dancing to some tired ass song, collect her fee and move on to the next fisted ten. He had a little more than ten dollars that night, so she took him in back to the VIP room for a private dance. It was the room where dirty dancing was given a whole new meaning, and if the tips were right, it was a room where almost anything could go. Her rate in the VIP room doubled per song, and if he paid her enough she'd even let him touch.

He was inexperienced with strip clubs — she could tell. He only had enough to see her dance, but not enough for a touch — and touching was the only reason men spent money to journey back there. So as his money ran out, toward the end of the final song, she thought she'd give him a taste of what he'd missed and maybe he'd spend more money on her if ever he returned. But when she sat backwards on his lap and pulled his arms around her breasts to let him squeeze, she felt a raw hunger in his hands, and when his mouth gently bit into the flesh on her back some dormant hunger awoke in her and shot up from between her legs. And before she knew what sense to make of it, she had let him lay her on her back across the VIP room's couch and she committed the first deadly sin of her trade … she kissed him. Deeply.

Dante licked, sucked, bit, and kissed all over her naked body. His tongue stroking her soft, supple skin as if she were covered in whipped cream. She grew wet from the inside out, her center dripped like melting ice. But when the tip of his finger touched her *there*, the light in her eyes came back on. Dante had pushed her panic button and when she came to her senses she pushed him off of her and threw him out of the room, but not before she collected the cash he owed her.

She'd come close to slipping before in that back room, but the risk was worth the money she could make for fulfilling fantasies at twenty dollars per song.

She thought that was the last of him, but Dante came back a week later and wanted more private dances. And each time a song ended he requested one more, and after ten songs had passed, she finally took a break. But when she whispered "that's two hundred dollars, Boo," in his ear he paid her with a poem. A poem! She unfolded his payment and all she saw was a feeble collection of words chicken scratched on college ruled paper. She was furious at him for playing her—fucking with her money and her time. So she let out a vile cacophony of profanity and called the bouncer over to clean him out. Dante got his ass beat that night; he was yanked out of his chair and carried out of the club, followed by two more bouncers looking to kick some ass. And it was a full hour later, after she deftly made her rounds and performed table dances to a few more songs, that she realized she still clutched the poem he used as payment. And when she read it she cried.

She ran outside the club donned in only her bikini and spiked heels screaming the name he signed at the bottom of her poem. She found him in the alley, propped against the wall of the club, his face swollen and bloody, his clothes all but torn off. She grabbed his face and met his eyes and heard him say, "I love you," before he passed out.

* * *

She couldn't wait to get home and shower the pungent cigarette smell of the club off her skin. Everything about exotic dancing finally repulsed her, but the money was so good she put her burgeoning morals aside. In the last few months of dancing at Pussykatz, it took every bit of her self-esteem not to feel cheapened by the groping stares from the legion of faceless men who came there to be aroused. It was wonderful at first, because she was making money off of them, but when the money started making her, she lost touch within herself. That's why Dante's poem touched her so deeply. She'd finally met a man who saw more than just a naked body. For, once upon a time, she'd considered exotic dancing an art, and the exhibition of it, a craft. But no one seemed to notice and even fewer cared. All anyone at the club wanted to see was tits and ass. And soon, she stopped caring too ... but Dante's poem had brought her back to Life.

*   *   *

Sheron emerged from the pedestrian tunnel of the subway and walked briskly home. When she rounded the corner to her brownstone, she found Dante sitting at her door. They spoke with their eyes, which read an exchange of cold hellos. Sheron ignored him, stepping around him like a forgotten trash bag left out for collection, put the key in the lock, and closed the door on his back.

Chapter Six
Naked Truths

"**S**o aren't you going to say hello?" she asked, sliding onto the stool beside him.

The man knew who she was before he looked at her. He turned to the eyes that had singled him out of the many and flirted with him across the room for the past thirty minutes. He smiled into them and took another sip of his drink.

"You know, it's not nice to stare … unless you're going to say hello."

"Hello." He finally found his voice, thanks to the two shots he'd downed quickly and the cognac he now nursed, trying to swig enough courage elixir to go over to her. Now, here she was on the stool beside him.

"Hi," she said. Her smile was warm. And sexy. But then, everything about her was. She was tiny, but curved. Very nicely curved. One of those petitely built women that made you feel like you could throw her over your shoulder, but if you did you'd fear breaking her. The way she looked at him, though, he got the feeling she didn't fear a thing.

His eyes roamed up from her knee-high black boots, to the invitingly short and tight skirt, to the pewter colored silk blouse that was only using two of its five buttons. He dared not look at the full lips she kept licking, nervously betraying her outer poise. They were much too tempting. Instead, he fixed his gaze on safer ground and looked through the tight curls of the brown, shoulder-length hair that sometimes fell into her face and shielded one of those eyes that not only stared at him intently, but flashed messages he dared not believe were meant for him.

"What's your name?" she continued.

"Are you picking me up?" He surprised himself. He didn't usually get so bold so quickly. But the green light was so damn bright he was losing his doubt and assuming the role of the movie hero, acting confidently because the script had his back.

"Do you want me to?"

Her empty glass gave him a way to dodge her quick comeback. He hadn't read the whole script yet. He went for tried and true, "Can I buy you another drink?"

"Are you picking me up?"

Damn, she was nobody's understudy.

"I'm just being polite," he lied.

"Are you always this polite to everyone you meet in a bar?"

"No, just the beautiful women with big, brown eyes, wearing sexy little outfits."

She smiled and said, "Give me a screaming orgasm."

"What?" He almost fell off his stool.

She threw her head back and laughed with delight. "That's what I'm drinking, a screaming orgasm."

He had to laugh with her. He ordered the orgasm, another cognac for himself.

"So what's in a screaming orgasm?" he asked her as the bartender put the creamy, white liquid on the bar.

"You don't know?" She smiled.

"You want to show me?" He was starting to feel confidence that had nothing to do with liquor.

"If you promise to be a good student."

"I'm much better when I'm bad." Another tired line, but it worked—her tantalizing smile remained. It had such promise in it.

"So what's your name bad-boy, or is it some major secret?" she asked, licking her lips again. Maybe it wasn't a nervous action.

"Eric. And yours?" He was completely relaxed now. It was on. He felt his excitement rising to match his interest as he began to let his imagination loose.

"Anike." Her name slid out just as smoothly.

"Anike," he repeated softly.

"Yes. So what's your game?"

Game? She caught him off guard … again. How do you answer that question? Though he talked like he did, he had never believed he had game, but her sitting beside him all intent and interested must mean something. Still, he didn't know if it was something you owned up to—if you really had it that is. He tried to duck again, "Why do you think I'm throwing you game?"

"Isn't everyone here?" She waved a hand around the room. He suddenly became reacquainted with the room and its occupants, each of whom he had become completely oblivious to since she had sat beside him. The close quarters of the small neighborhood joint with tables, chairs, stools, and bodies crammed into every spare change of space no longer needed to alleviate the loneliness he still felt a year after receiving his final divorce decree. The beats of the house music he had been silently begging them to change and the voices trying to talk over it had become the soundtrack for the movie unfolding on their stools.

She went on, "Why else would anyone spend time and energy in a place like this, where everyone's tongue is befriended by alcohol, a drink can buy you company, and regardless of who assumes the role of hunter or prey, everyone knows what prize they're playing for?"

He swallowed painfully. Was she seeing through his cool?

Though they had gotten a little pensive, her smiling eyes hadn't changed. As he watched her, he realized she was thinking about something or someone—but for those moments, he wasn't it.

Then, just like that, she snapped out of it and moved on, dismissing her introspection with a quick wave. "Plus, it's dark, noisy, and stinks with alcohol and smoke." She started laughing at a private joke, then shared it. "But don't get me on a soapbox or anything," she smiled. "Must be the liquor."

He didn't care what it was. He was just glad he was sitting there in the front row saying amen to her every word: noise, smoke, and all.

"And what's your game?" He redirected the conversation to its previous intimate track.

"You first, Ricky."

"Eric."

"Ricky," her eyes flashed. Daring him.

He was about to correct her again when he realized it didn't matter what she called him. He would answer. The thought almost made him kiss her. He came to his senses just in time and stopped himself. Then he did something equally crazy. He stood up and took her hand. It was intense standing so close to her, and it fueled him before the doubts took over. He hadn't felt this comfortable with a woman in a long time. He hadn't talked this way with a woman even longer. His body screamed at him how easy this was, and reminded him how much self-doubt had controlled his tongue and feet every time someone stirred his interest recently. His newly charged ego looked down at her upturned face. She wore a lazy, knowing smile. "Come home with me, Anike," he heard his ego say.

"Not yet," she promised. She removed her hand from his and placed it on his chest. She gently pushed him back onto his stool and reminded him who had the lead role, sliding her hand deliberately down his chest and teasingly down one thigh. The threads in his denim jeans seemed to pop as her finger traced its path. Knowing her hand had his attention, she removed it and slowly stroked the letters "y-e-s" into the condensation on her glass. The promise threw the final snare into him. Then she simply reiterated, "Not yet."

* * *

The night had gotten a lot cooler than when she had strutted out earlier, full of confidence in her shield of black and pewter, feeling smooth, and prowling like a cat. A half smile had dangled off her lips as she noticed the men who turned and watched her ass switch, without really seeing them. She just knew they would. She had been working the attitude.

But now, as she walked with her head down, arms tightly wrapped around herself in the crisp night air, the cat-titude that had clung to her shoulders like a warm, well-worn coat was gone. Killed with a single shot blazing from something she couldn't fully read in the bartender's eyes. Was it pity? She couldn't put her finger on what it was. But it tore into her, stripped away the black cat shield thing and exposed her.

Ricky—Eric had excused himself and gone to the bathroom right after they'd ordered another round. At first, she sat there laughing with herself imagining just what he really needed to do in there. She knew men sometimes did things to help them last longer in bed. It amused her that he didn't realize that minuteman or energizer bunny, his hand was the only one that would ever know the difference tonight.

But when the bartender's slow, deliberate motion made her look into his eyes as he pushed another screaming orgasm towards her, she knew she would choke on it if she took the first sip. Her snicker froze in midair and clattered to the ground with her shield as he undressed her, read her, and reflected what he saw. And she looked at herself. Looked at herself like everybody else around her probably did.

Why wouldn't he look at her with pity? Or was it scorn? How many times had he seen her in there flirting unabashedly with some man she'd just met? She'd been there with that other guy last weekend. The one with the dreadlocks and the African name. When she'd let him stroke her inner thigh a few times, she knew he would have sat right there at the bar while the last boat sailed back to Africa. She could have called him Toby and he would have whimpered, "Yes."

She now realized that visiting the same few places for the extra level of confidence they provided was a novice's mistake. She had played herself as much as she'd played all those men, trying to compete in a game she only knew about from being on the losing end.

Now on instant replay, she relived all her fumbles. She saw the many times the same bouncer had seen her dry hump some desperate puppy in the middle of the dance floor. She relived the moment when the DJ had the crowd up and grooving and everybody else was yelling, "Play that jam, oh yes, that's the shit," and she had had some brother irrational and pleading, "Oh yes, oh yes, please, don't stop," his groin begging to reach some other symphony.

It was unrecoverable. She knew that. Nobody knew that she hadn't slept with any of them. That she would turn them on, but never turn them out. That she left them hanging on to promises she whispered into their thirsty ears. Promises of chances to be with her that evaporated with the rising temperature she created. And would it matter if the bartender, or the bouncer, or the DJ, or the waitress, or anyone knew that she hadn't fucked them? Hadn't fucked anyone since Derek left? Would that make her any less trifling?

As she hurried from the bar, she wanted to hide from the people on the street. Fortunately, at three ten in the morning none of the stragglers stopped to inquire of the single woman clad in black and pewter, "Why are you crying?" Many of them would cry too if they were walking the street alone at that hour.

She couldn't get alone enough. Away from their pitying eyes—no less hurtful than those of the bartender. As exposed as she felt, she knew even these strangers might see through her. She begged her shame to cover her as her cat-titude had earlier, but instead it danced mockingly in front of her, showing her snapshots of the men she'd hurt over the past few months.

When the review of her recently sordid history caught up with tonight's fiasco, she imagined the look that must have been on Eric's face when he came out of the bathroom and found her gone. Somehow she had never thought about it before. Now, she could feel the impact of her callous actions just like Derek was walking out on her again. And she remembered too, that she had worn that very look. She'd worn it so long that it remained, even when she could only remember the music his fingers made by playing one of his CDs.

The bitter memory of the time when he used to burn CDs just for her and take her to his shows gripped her as sobs shook her body. Lying in bed beside her, he would listen intently while she gave her opinion of his songs. She had thought *her* opinion really mattered. She hadn't known it was just a part of the daily diet his ego needed.

It took all that waiting for him to return for her to understand that as long as he had those guitar strings he would always play her like a mistress. "I've been busy, baby, that's why I didn't call." Or, "I'll be gone as long as I need to be gone. You know this is how I make my living." It didn't have anything to do with making a living, that guitar was his world. When she had waited around to get equal status with a hollowed out piece of wood and six strings of wire, she'd felt exactly what Eric and the others had experienced when they looked for her in the dust of her sudden exits. That was the real team she played on. She hadn't changed sides just by wearing a new uniform.

Mentally whipping herself, she was completely unprepared when she heard a familiar voice break through her curtain of tears. She panicked, thinking it was the same voice that had been whispering and licking her ear some twenty minutes ago. Slowly, she turned and realized which night this voice had tickled her ears.

As Dante uncurled from the brownstone stoop he'd been sitting on and came towards her with a confused look on his face, she begged for wings. For black, rainbow-tipped butterfly wings to sprout from that place in her back that was paralyzed with tension. If she could have moved, she would have flapped her arms to see if her prayers were answered. Instead, she fought to control her facial expression, hoping to appear calm and cool. Shit, she forgot she had been crying for close to forever.

"Cia? What's up? Hey ... what's wrong?"

What was wrong was the name she had given him in the club that night. What was wrong was that his first words were concern for her when she had played him for a fool, used him like a tool and hung up on his climax. But perhaps he was also reeling from this inconceivable meeting and soon would recall his right to regard her as the bitch she'd been.

She attempted to recapture the cat stance, the cat moves, the cat-titude. But her wavering, hoarse voice let her know it wasn't going to happen when all she could force out was, "Not much."

Not only was the attitude gone, she had been disrobed of her witty replies and sexual innuendoes. Not one thing came to her but the truth. And she hadn't made peace with it yet.

"Damn, if this ain't a small world. Man, I never thought I'd run into you again." His attempt to strike up an even, casual conversation died with his allusion to their previous meeting. No longer hidden behind the telephone, his smooth as butter, booty-call making attitude had run out on him as well, and was probably spread all over the same sidewalks where she had left her ocean of tears. Or maybe she had killed it when the connection went dead in his hand the night they met.

"Look," she took a deep breath, "my name's not Cia,"

"Huh?"

She tried to brush it off lightly, "It … that was just a club thing, you know? Not Cia, not Anike, not Grace, not Seraph … " she trailed off and watched for his reaction. "It's Eliza."

The furrows on his forehead deepened, though he only nodded slightly and said, "Oh." She knew he didn't quite know what to make of what he was hearing. He was probably trying to figure out which lie was really a lie.

"Ah," she tried, "do you live around here? I thought you said you lived … " She realized a little too late the part she must have played in his sitting alone on a stoop at three thirty in the morning. It was surely testament to the disposition of the woman who had scrutinized them intently as they worked it on the dance floor. And this was obviously the closest thing to a doghouse the neighborhood had to offer.

"No, I, ah … "

She could see he was battling between a lie and the truth. "I'm … I was going to see Sheron. You know … " She gave him credit for taking the high road, but wished he would make up a lie that could send them both on their way.

She looked away. So dagger-lady's name was Sheron. It was only now that Eliza felt the wounds of the knives Sheron must have plunged repeatedly into her back as Eliza brought Dante to dancefloor climax after climax right beneath her seething eyes. The only thing she had felt at the time was Dante's groin moaning against hers and his hands talking excitedly to any part of her body she let him meet.

"I had a dream, a nightmare … and I … well, I always talk to her about … " he stopped and took his turn to avert his eyes as she looked at him with the "don't give me that stupid shit," look. She knew he was probably telling the truth again, but it was also obvious that what he went to see Sheron about, and what he ended up doing with her were two different things. She still had enough player-tude left to know that.

"You live around here?" The doubt resonated in his voice. He obviously had no idea what to believe. From what she'd said that night, her apartment should be on the other side of the hub of bars and clubs that bordered the neighborhood they stood in.

Eliza had to look around to get a good grip of where she really was. The neighborhood was familiar, but definitely not home. "No, I was … I was wandering. I just needed to walk. To think for a while … I didn't realize where I was walking because I—"

"—was crying." Their eyes met as Dante finished Eliza's sentence softly. "Why?" He actually dared to go there. "Something to do with your fiancé?"

Eliza gave him even more credit for that one.

"No," she shook her head. She started to reveal more, but stopped and instead said, "I gotta go." Her battered spirit had had enough truth tonight.

"Wait," he said, stopping her as she attempted to swiftly step past him and head away in the direction she had come from. He couldn't bear to be hung up on again. Something was beginning to nag at him about this second chance meeting. "I, ah," he searched for something smart to say and the gods shone upon him, "let me help you get a cab."

Her first instinct was to say no, but she knew she really shouldn't keep walking by herself that late. Especially with the footprints of her tears treading through the remains of the makeup on her face. She almost bowed her head, embarrassed at how awful she must look, especially in contrast to the image he had seen last time.

"Thanks," she agreed. Plus, she owed him that much. Though a walk was clearly not what he'd thought he was getting the last time they spoke.

They turned and began retracing her steps. Walking together silently, heading back towards the nightlife where cabbies would be hanging around waiting for drunken revelers who needed to be carted home. Dante was just sinking into a mind boggling recap of the strange interactions they'd had, while trying to decide if there was any safe topic of discussion he could bring up, when a window was violently thrown open upstairs in one of the brownstones behind them.

They both stopped. They were only a few feet back past Sheron's stoop; Eliza stared at the ground while Dante turned around. She already knew what there was to see.

When Dante didn't say anything, Sheron yelled at him, oblivious to the relations she was ruining with her neighbors, "Dante, what the fuck is going on? Where the hell you going?"

"I'm going to get her a cab."

Eliza almost laughed at his honesty.

"What? What the hell is that no-class ho doing outside my house? You think this is some joke or something? This is bullshit, Dante. Bullshit! I can't believe you trying this trifling shit on me. What am I supposed to be? Jealous?"

"We just ran into each other … "

It was the truth, but Eliza knew the truth wasn't going to solve everything tonight. Some things would take a little longer. She touched Dante's arm. "I'm going to go."

"No," he turned towards her, "I'll walk you to the cabs."

"I'm going to be just fine. She," Eliza motioned with her head to Sheron who was still hanging out her window and screaming at him, more angry now that they seemed to be ignoring her, "may not be. You need to go talk to her."

Dante turned and looked at Sheron. It was going to be a while before anyone could get a word through to her. But he had to wait it out. There were things to be dealt with. Things between him and Sheron and Eva and … damn, he stopped and thought about all the women he was naming. When did he end up with so many women problems? And now there was even Eliza, who kismet kept throwing at him.

He sighed and accepted his fate. Only one dragon could be slayed at a time. "Be careful, okay."

"You, too."

They almost smiled. Her wit was back. But it came from a different place. She felt her spirits picking themselves off the ground.

Eliza began walking down the sidewalk. She heard the quieter voice of Dante being raised, trying to get itself heard over the yelling Sheron as she refused to let him into the brownstone. It pleased her that he didn't have a key.

Suddenly, an impulse took her. She turned and yelled, "Dante!"

Both he and Sheron turned to look at her. From half a block away, Eliza admitted, "I don't have a fiancé."

"What?"

"I don't have a fiancé. He left me a year ago. I just got over him. Tonight."

Dante stared at her with his mouth hanging open. What the hell did that mean?

Sheron had had enough. "Fuck you, Dante, I don't need this shit. You just a triflin' ass motherfucker. I don't know why I ever bothered with you. I knew you would be nothin' but trouble. You … you and your fuckin' poem an' shit." She only stopped when she realized he wasn't even looking at her, just staring down the block at Eliza.

By the time Dante heard Sheron through the fog of thoughts that smothered him with Eliza's words, she had slammed the window. And drawn her blinds. When he looked back down the block, Eliza was gone.

Chapter Seven
Flicker in the Night

Nothingness. That was what he was left with. The woman that he thought he wanted, didn't want him, the woman that he wanted just for want's sake didn't know how to be wanted, and the woman that he wanted and had, he'd thrown away by accident. At that moment, he thought, it might be easier to just be the dog that Malik was. Malik's motto was "Fuck 'em." Just the saying the phrase would send Malik into fits of laughter.

Dante, "the thinker," as Malik called him, would spend hours trying to decide if that meant, "fuck them" like "fuck that," synonymous with "don't even sweat 'em," or "fuck them," like "just hit it and quit it," which Dante was ashamed to admit, was the outcome of most of his sexual encounters.

The thing that Malik clowned him about most was that Dante actually took the time to feel bad about it. Which always led him to do something stupid like call the women back—or send them a note, a rose, or a damned poem (look what a mess that had made with Sheron). Then, after that, it was always back on, and it took months of mercy sex, apologies and "ghetto scenes" to finally turn it off.

Women had been a source of confusion and awkwardness from day one for him. He recalled some of the stories his parents told of his innocent yet unusual encounters with women. As a four-year-old, he accidentally pulled a woman's bikini top off as she was holding him and saying how adorable he was. He could still remember the burn of his eyes as they nearly popped out of their sockets as he saw for the first time what created the "bumps" in his mother's top. The large mounds of flesh that fell out of the bikini top stayed on his mind for years. His knee still smarted slightly at the pain that it felt when he hit the sand after the woman dropped him and ran in embarrassment. He remembered watching her run away and wanting to see more. He remembered having flashes of that moment for years and years. As a six-year-old, he slipped and fell into a woman's lap on the bus. He remembered his hand slipping from the bus pole and grasping for something to hold him up. His hand hit her knee and he thought he was safe but it fell immediately into the fabric between her opened knees. He felt himself falling further, grabbed for something and ended up with his hands between her legs. She'd jumped up and made him fall to the floor of the bus, leaving him in a heap—to the amusement of everyone stuck in rush hour traffic. His father had rushed to pick him up, laughing and patting him on the head. "My boy, my boy, my boy," was all his father could say about it.

Women had always had that effect on him. And even now as a grown man, he was still slipping and falling and ending up in awkward places—not knowing where to put his hands. He smiled thinking of how hard it is to escape yourself.

He gave Sheron's window one last glance for confirmation that it was over, picked up his battered ego and started walking the same direction Eliza had walked. He was hoping not to see her. If he did see her, he planned to call her a "lying, holdin' out bitch." Or, he would tell her that he understands the webs people weave—and then he'd offer to go have coffee with her and they'd sit up all night talking about the difficulty of human connection amongst the "liars and thieves." That was the name he had for all the people out there struggling for love, like himself. He would probably confess after about three cups, that he lied a lot too.

He would then explain that his personal brand of lies was not about things like his name or occupation, but about who he really was and what he really wanted. He would leave it at that, not going into the fact that the main victim of his lies was himself. He would keep it simple so that she would feel at ease, connected and possibly in the mood to go back to his two rooms and give him some. That would be helpful to him when Malik called for the "weekend in review," as he called it. It would give him something to say, so he'd stop fucking with him about his "sob stories" and his "hit and miss moments."

He thought he wanted a relationship. That was what Eva and Sheron had been for. Filling that slot. Eva's innocence and complete willingness to love him so hard, scared him. Sheron, on the other hand, seemed more like it. She was fly as hell, not innocent at all, and not easy to handle. He realized that he was a glutton for pain. Through both of these encounters, Malik teased him, but Dante knew he was jealous as hell.

In both cases, time crawled, yet sped by and before he had time to protest, they had become his girlfriends and started to feel like obligations that never set right. He was always questioning it, himself and her. With Sheron he always questioned her dancing career, her honesty and her secrecy. With Eva, he wondered why such an innocent girl would choose to give it all up to him. With Sheron, he had told her everything. He had told her about losing his parents when he was young and how bad that fucked with him, and how he sometimes cried when he saw Martin Luther King, Jr. images or heard one of those "damned speeches" that they play on TV in February. He told her a lot, but she never gave up any information about her past, unlike Eva who had told him far more than he wanted to know after only three days. Sheron just talked about the fancy house and bank account she wanted by the time she was thirty-five. The shit that she knew he could never give her with his social work career.

He did have one secret left. The one thing that he never shared with Sheron or Eva was how much he realized that he never really had people in his life that he felt he could trust. And how he grew up hating his "boys" for most of the time he had known them. In fact, he didn't even know how they had crashed into his life so hard. He had grown up with the kids on the block and the next thing he knew, he was comparing dick sizes and how many women they'd had. It was like he had missed the screening process—the time to decide if he even liked these people. Respected them. Trusted them.

He never forgot the time that Lo (short for Lorenzo) had stole the pretty honey from down south, the one that he told him and everyone else that he liked. He had meant it.

She had come to visit her aunt who lived in the building. Her name was Francine but everyone called her France. France had honey colored skin and hazel eyes. Dante had never seen a girl with eyes like that. All he could do is stare into them whenever she'd walk up to him with her I'm-sexy-and-don't-I-know-it walk and her homemade smile and say, "Hey Dantayyyy." He could rarely get out more than a quiet, "What's up?" Her lips were the reddest lips he had ever seen and he still wished he had gotten the chance to bite into them; taste the cherry juice that must have been inside.

He had gotten to be friendly with her—but was too scared to let her know how he really felt. He would just speak and be cordial and talk to her about passing things like what she was doing that day and when was she going back home. He spent many hours that summer dreaming of talking to her for real, touching her hair, removing her bleached white training bra … but that's not what he told his boys. He just told them that she was fine. And that he'd do her if given the chance.

That's what they all said about every girl on the block, so no one took it seriously, and that's why everyone was surprised when he went off because he found France and Lo kissing in the stairwell. What he did was so bad that he didn't even like to think about it anymore. He was surprised at himself. Never knew he had that kind of strength, passion, and venom flowing through his veins. France left town to go home the next day, and he still didn't know if it was because of how he acted or because school was starting again. As far as Lo was concerned—it was never the same again. Even now. They were cool with each other in passing, but nothing like they had been. Dante heard that Lo had called him a punk after that. Dante never called Lo anything except for his well-earned nickname.

He lost his trust that summer. And even though Lo was the only one who ever crossed him like that, it was never the same with any of those guys, because he could see from their eyes they all would have done what Lo did. He tried hard to distance himself from them. Making excuses when they were going to hang or grub. He eventually saw less and less of them. But no matter how hard he tried, he just couldn't shake Malik. Kind of like family. He came from where he did. He looked the way he did. He lived the way he did, so it was too late. He was affiliated. Stuck.

Stuck was how he felt tonight. Stuck in limbo. Not bad, not good. Not mad, not glad. Just there—not exactly sure what to do next. Eliza must have turned down a side street because there wasn't a trace of her anywhere. Actually, it's for the better, he thought.

It was a clear, still night and although it was late, there was energy in the air. Or maybe it was his restlessness disguised as energy dancing around him. He walked aimlessly into the park and decided to sit and wait for a sign. He had nothing to gain and nothing to lose. He remembered his religious grandmother used to always say, "Baby, when you don't know what to do—just wait for a sign. He'll give you one." She never explained what the sign would look or feel like. She always said, "When it comes, you'll know." Dante never forgot that about her, even though she had passed away years ago. He hoped that perhaps this was when the truth came out, or at least the signs. He entered the dark park and chose a bench near the entrance, under a dim light. There, he could disappear in darkness and wait in peace.

The sweet and sour smell of dog and human urine wafted up from around the bench reminding him that life reeked. He reveled in the smell while it turned his growling stomach. He grabbed a newspaper that sat at his feet and picked it up. The headlines were two days old, but he had not seen a paper in weeks, so even old news would be news to him.

He was reading a stained article about healthcare for poor folks, or the lack thereof, when he noticed the silhouette of a woman nervously approaching the bench across the way. It was smack dab under a street lamp. She had chin length locks and moved with a certain grace that rang painfully familiar. Her body was wide but beautiful. Her simple beauty was magnificent. He felt something familiar, but couldn't place it. She looked around as if she was waiting for someone and Dante wished it were him.

No one came for a few minutes and she spent the time looking at her watch, trying to be occupied with the intricacies of its design. Dante wanted to get her attention but thought it would be wiser to see whom she was waiting for and why. It was the middle of the night; she wasn't out there for nothing.

* * *

She could feel his presence and thought perhaps she should move to another bench, but there was no other bench with as bright a light. It was safer under the light. Plus, she didn't want to appear as scared as she was.

The night grew so quiet that she thought she could hear him breathing. She didn't want him to think she was scared. She could hold her own, if he were going to start something. To pass time she imagined warm breath on the back of her neck. She imagined its moist heat making the hairs on her back dance. She imagined a swollen tongue lightly flicking her neck and strong hands crawling down the front of her jacket, seeking her breasts, hungrily. A dog's bark in the distance brought her back and only two minutes had passed. She was getting impatient. The waiting was the most excruciating part.

She slowly turned her head toward him. His head was buried in a crumpled newspaper—but she knew he was watching. Men always did. His outline showed that he had long, strong locks that fell below his broad shoulders. She was reminded of her last man's locks and how they had felt between her lips when he was over her, her mouth wide open with urgent ecstasy. He would let that one lone lock linger between her lips, lightly scratchy and ticklish on her tongue. She smiled just thinking about it.

It was getting late. She hated lateness. Suddenly this was a bad idea. She was out of her depth.

At that moment, out of nowhere, she felt real breath dancing on the back of her exposed neck. She closed her eyes and opened her mouth with a smile. She leaned her head back to greet the face of life-after-Dante, and squirmed with excitement.

* * *

Dante was intrigued and hoped they wouldn't mind if he watched. Maybe he would learn something. He could feel himself getting warm all over as if he had swallowed a lighted match. The heat moved gradually from his throat to his stomach, flaring out to the left and right to reach his hands, and aimed for his center. His palms started to sweat and his jeans felt tighter.

There was a thin, fair-skinned figure sitting behind the girl on the bench. His face was frail from what Dante could see. His head was covered by a wool knit cap. His frailty was unusual but the girl's face was glowing in his presence.

* * *

She heard, "Sorry I'm late," being whispered into her neck.

"It's okay," she said and pulled the figure around to her face.

* * *

Dante was shocked. It was a woman who had come to meet the girl.

* * *

"I hate lateness," the girl said honestly, though not wanting to sound offensive.

The stranger said, "I'm sorry I'm late. It was hard getting out tonight, but I wouldn't have missed it for the world."

They stared at each other for a moment. Neither one knowing what to do next. The girl stared into the face of her adventure and thought how beautiful the stranger was and how her voice didn't do her magical face justice.

She never thought she'd answer the ad in that paper. It was an innocent curiosity. She was actually picking it up to throw it away and the classified page just fell open. She had promised herself she would only read one. And she did. Then another. Then another, until she was sitting on the floor cross-legged in her white satin panties, moist with interest. She combed the MEN SEEKING MEN section hurriedly, trying not to admit that she was a WOMAN SEEKING anything at all. When she saw the black capital letters that announced her future, she read voraciously, happy to be in her own house, knowing it was just a private moment between she and herself. Knowing that reading this would have no impact on her public life. No one would have to know.

"Happily married, but consistently gay woman seeking curious young woman aged 20-25 with beauty, substance and hot sex on a platter. Box #222."

She had read it over and over until she could recite it like a poem. Then she looked around her empty apartment, picked her phone up from the floor and called the number. Her message had been brief, nervous, and breathy.

"Hello. I don't know what to say. I think I am those things. You tell me. 749-5916. Leave a message where you want to meet. Don't talk a lot. Anytime, I'll be there." She hung up shaking inside. Not knowing what to expect, but happy she had done it. Finally. Her thirst would be quenched. Since those unfortunate months in Jamaica, she'd been mad at herself for letting herself fall so deeply into Dante. She should have known from the start. He was a little strange. Not a long history of real relationships; an artist; and his parents had died early. All signs of an emotional fuck-up. She had known but didn't want to miss out on his words, his love of music, and his attempted sincerity. But he had hurt her deeply and she was through. Through with the man game. She thought women would be easier, closer to what she knew. Not as much guessing. The ad was going to be the beginning.

Today, she'd heard an unfamiliar voice on her voicemail. "Thanks for calling. Tonight. Eleven o'clock. The Park. The bench with the light. See ya."

She liked, "See ya." It was cool and casual. Friendly and warm. Familiar. She was glad she didn't even have enough time to change her mind or make up an excuse. Tonight was the night.

*　*　*

The stranger was pleasantly surprised. The girl on the bench was the most beautiful woman she had ever met from the newspaper ads. The stranger could see how scared she was. How new she was. And how straight. She couldn't wait to turn her world around. The new ones were always the best.

The stranger said, "I don't have much time, but I wish I had an eternity."

The girl was impressed by her willingness to be poetic under these circumstances. She felt the blood rush to her center. Her knees loosened and her head lightened.

The stranger moved in closely and said, "My name is Juliette." Eva said softly, "I'm Eva."

Juliette kissed the tip of her nose with the lightness of cotton. Eva shuddered with joy and stuck her tongue out to meet her new lover's smooth lips. Her kisses were like angels floating from her neck to her collarbone to her breastbone. Eva felt her blouse being opened and didn't even care. She could feel the eyes of the guy on the bench and she still didn't care. She could feel herself falling back as her hand fought to get into the tiny space between her body and Juliette's. She found the zipper of her own jeans and jerkily unzipped them — freeing herself up for ecstasy.

* * *

Dante could feel his interest growing. Never before had he seen such a scene. He was having a hard time containing himself. Trying to find a way to touch himself without looking like he was, he pulled the stained newspaper over his lap and slid back on his bench, further into darkness, surprised at the power of arousal. His brain ached with confusion and envy, while his body pulsated with excitement. He couldn't help his hand as it independently found its way to his crotch.

The newspaper rattled at his movement and his senses were so heightened that it sounded like firecrackers cracking. He stopped suddenly to make sure the girl and her lover had not been disturbed. He licked his own lips, wishing it were him getting busy under the moonlight with someone with whom he had a connection.

* * *

Juliette's hands became more forceful as they reached the Eva's breasts. She caressed their roundness first, then dove towards them with a wide, wet mouth. She took one breast and then another; sucking and teasing each one. Eva sighed and began to groan. Her eyes closed as if she had left her body and gone to heaven, lightly pulling Juliette behind her. Juliette smiled as her kisses covered Eva's chest. Her own body was warming up now and she wanted to love Eva more. She reached down to Eva's opened zipper and found a layer of coarse hair there to meet her. She slid two curious fingers down Eva's pelvic bone until she felt the plushness of her interior begin to open.

* * *

Dante was impressed and jealous at his own inability to make a woman feel so good.

* * *

Eva had left her body. Her mind had taken her to the place it always goes when she wants to have the deepest implosions. It went back to Jamaica and Dante's hard chest and demanding hands. She found herself back beneath his powerful hips noisily beating against hers, pumping her with charged adrenaline. Dante had always been wrong for her. Too young, too troubled and too scared. But it was his strong hands and nasty ways that had gotten her addicted. And although he caused her pain, he had introduced her to passion and for that she was forever grateful.

She said his name over and over in her head like a mantra, straining not to gratefully scream it out to the gods. She watched the Technicolor Dante love scene intently as it flickered in her mind. She felt her juices building in response to Juliette's physical work and her fond memories of Dante; both working in tandem to bring her nearer to the point of a sublime electric shock.

* * *

Sweat poured down Dante's face, which curled with pleasure. His hand worked and jerked down below his tensed stomach, while the stained newspaper slid to the ground. He was soon to reach the place that he had hoped he would reach tonight—shameless bliss. His hardened self was twitching within his fingers with expectation and he knew the moment of truth was near.

He opened one eye to see the outline of the girl's form. That would get him there. His half-open eye could only see her slender neck. Her head was thrown into the darkness.

* * *

By now, Juliette's knees were on the cement and her head was buried in Eva's lap. She inhaled Eva's nectar and felt faint. It was a scent like she had never known. Sweet and clean with innocence, yet ripe and pungent with desire. Her mouth dripped with anticipation of Eva's stickiness the second before she let herself taste it.

Juliette's heart was pounding when she finally rose from her knees. She suddenly felt like crying. She had never been able to give this kind of pleasure in the past. She loved Eva for being so open and coming to her affection so willingly, but she had to get back to her husband. It would soon be time to go.

* * *

Dante gave a final thrust between his fingers and the warm stickiness began to drip down his hands and onto his denim. He let out a silent sigh of relief as the girl and her lover sat on the bench and laughed warmly. They smoothed each other's hair and giggled in that way that only girlfriends can.

In a groggy state, he noticed the stained newspaper lying at his feet, not serving the purpose for which it was intended. He had been exposed. He saw the girl kiss the neck of her lover and regretfully turn towards the park's exit.

* * *

Juliette waved to Eva knowing that she would never see her again.

* * *

Eva waved back to Juliette, moved by her own lust and eagerness for a next time.

* * *

Dante looked at them both, suddenly realizing that the girl was not a figment of his lust. The girl leaving the park was Eva. His Eva.

Chapter Eight
Moments of Truth

"Rough day at work, huh?"

Dante had been absorbed with thoughts about one of his clients. Chantrise, a nineteen-year-old with two children who was about to be thrown out onto the street. It hurt sometimes, his job did. He got into social work to help people, but the red tape was more and more impossible to cut through. It entangled his clients in hopelessness and then sealed them there. He was getting tired.

All the way home he worked on getting his optimism to kick in, but there was a odd feeling—a pain, a weariness settling into him. Life was strange. Everything was a mess: his job, his relationships, his friendships, even his mind—a fucking mess.

Malik asked him a question a few days ago that really shook him. Dante should have known the conversation would be deep. Malik called to invite him to lunch. "It's on me," he'd said. Malik rarely had time to do lunch and when he made the time, something serious was happening.

"Everything a'ight, man?" Dante asked. Although Malik assured him that things were cool and he just wanted to hang out, Dante knew that there was something important on his friend's mind. Later that afternoon over roti, rice, beans, and plantains, after all the talk of hip-hop, basketball, and work was exhausted, Malik got to the heart of the matter.

"How long have we been boys, Dante?"

"Forever, man. Why you wanna celebrate our anniversary?" Dante asked laughing.

Malik rolled his eyes and smiled. "Man, I've known you for a minute and …," he got quiet, which was very rare for Malik, "and the shit you've been doing lately … it's not like you." Malik looked at Dante intently. "I'm asking you this as a friend, Dante: Who are you trying to be? Where are you going with your shit?"

Something inside Dante shifted. He felt as though the air in the room was clogged. He coughed, ran his hand through his locks, looked down at his hands, looked at his friend, looked him in the eyes. It seemed as though he hadn't looked in anyone's eyes for a while.

He wanted to curse Malik out. Ask, "Who the fuck are you and where are you going with yo' shit?" But he saw no meanness in Malik's face, so he couldn't summon up any in himself. The thing inside him kept shifting, he started blinking hard, he was keeping something back and he was starting to see it. All the shit he'd been keeping down about his job, his boys, his women, his parents.

He was tired of fighting, tired of burying, tired of drowning, forgetting, and sweeping under the rug. So he did the only thing a grown, hurting black man could do in public when he finally let himself feel the stings. He laughed. He laughed loud and hard and long. Malik was his friend, Malik was a man, Malik studied psychology, Malik understood and he nodded and said, "Man, everything's gonna be all right."

Dante hadn't felt the same after that. The last few days, it felt like the ground was giving way under his feet. The nights brought dreams of speeding cars and his mother trying to dodge them. He saw himself in the mirror and wondered about his reflection; he'd been feeling like even his hair was heavy. He vaguely remembered the man he was when he started his locks two years ago. A different man. He just wanted to be himself. He knew what he needed.

"Yeah, rough day," he said to Treasure who was on his stoop with a turquoise gift bag and five sunflowers in her arms. She looked radiant. Radiant in a way he'd never seen before. Her hair covered in a pink gauze headwrap, her long white dress flowing in the breeze, silver bracelets from wrists to elbows and a translucent pink scarf worn loose around her shoulders. He was struck by the sight of her. They hadn't seen each other in at least a month and a half.

"These are for you," she said handing him the sunflowers awkwardly.

He was stunned. "For me?"

He invited her in. She slipped her sandals off and sat on his burgundy beanbag. Dante put his bag down, still puzzled by the flowers. He put them in the only vase he had. It was a gigantic and purple and had belonged to his mother.

"Iced tea, water of sorrel?" he asked.

"Oh, a brotha got somethin' in his fridge now?" Treasure joked. "Iced tea sounds good." He chuckled, brought their glasses into the living room and took a seat across from her. She sipped her tea and spoke first.

"So we haven't exactly been good to each other have we?"

"No," Dante offered slowly, "we haven't."

"We haven't been too good to ourselves either. I've decided to stop treating myself like shit. I named myself Treasure to remind myself that I am one. And I still forget." She paused to finish off her iced tea. "This past year was drama and deception. I like you, Dante. Leaving my drawers around your crib and sneaking out in the middle of the night wasn't the way to show it. Giving you ass indiscriminately wasn't the way either, and I know this now. We used each other. I want to be your friend but I gotta be my own friend first. I came here to give you the flowers and this." She handed him the turquoise bag.

Treasure was full of surprises. Their relationship had fallen apart and here she was sharing truth and offering gifts. He reached in and took out a journal with a large cliff and an ocean on the cover. He sighed.

"What did I do to deserve this? I've been an asshole," he shrugged.

"We both have been," she corrected.

They sat silent for a moment. Dante studied the journal in his hand, the cover reminded him of Jamaica. He put the book down carefully.

"You're amazing," Dante said shaking his head. He had completely written Treasure off. In his mind she was another mistake he'd made. He had a long list of fuck-ups that he was only now starting to examine. Dante looked at Treasure. He looked at her dimpled chin, her full, curvy mouth, her regal nose and finally, her eyes. How many times had he and Treasure cheated sleep—breathless, sheets twisted rope-like, backs arching, brown caressing brown, and his eyes avoiding hers. So many times his eyes had avoided hers.

"What have I been thinking?" he said, his voice suddenly unsure and heavy. Heavy like the weight of all his unanswered questions. He looked into Treasure's eyes and inexplicably he felt as if he'd been behind walls and layers and he needed to breathe. To reach out. He ran his hand through his locks.

"I don't even know what to say, Treasure. Except that I've been trippin' and I'm sorry." She reached for his hand.

"It's okay—" she began.

"No. I've been an asshole and you need to know that this is not the real me." The air was thick and still. Dante looked at their hands for what seemed like an eternity. Holding Treasure's hand felt natural, warm, and secure. He thought suddenly about how his mother used to hold his hand and sing to him when he cried. He thought about how he held her hand that last time in the church and he waited for her to sing and how it was only when she didn't that he understood. He thought about this and almost by accident said, "Moms wouldn't be too thrilled with this bullshit."

Treasure grabbed his other hand and looked him gently in the eyes. "Listen, your mother loves you and she's proud that you are where you are. No, she wasn't thrilled. Not with the whole stripper thing, or the friends you've been keeping. She hated that shit in the park two weeks ago. But she loves you and you're on the right track now. Even though you feel like hell, you're on the path. Just remember that."

Dante decided not to ask Treasure how she knew what she knew. He was stunned in the first place, even though he'd had a feeling that she dealt with lots of other realms. He had a feeling that their episode was a momentary lapse. A human foible for a supernatural woman. For the first time he noticed the wine colored beads around her neck. He smiled.

"Thank you."

Treasure released his hands. "Hey darling, I've got to go. My plane is leaving in a few hours."

"Plane?"

"Yeah, I'm going to Brazil."

"What? How long?"

"Three months. Dance program. I'll send you some postcards."

For a moment Dante felt deflated because she was leaving. He felt connected to her for the first time. He knew she would send him postcards though, and he knew they would become friends when she returned.

"Amazing," he said, almost to himself.

She stood up to leave. "Thank you, Treasure," he said softly as they hugged.

"Do me a favor," she whispered in his ear, "write in that journal. Promise me you'll do it. Promise me you'll do it tonight."

"I will. I promise."

With that, Treasure slipped her sandals back on, floated out the door, down the steps, and into the hot August evening.

Dante headed to the bathroom. He took a long shower and thought about the moments of truth he'd been facing lately. He stepped out of the shower, wiped the mirror clear of steam. He examined himself. Ran a hand through his locks again. It was a strange gesture, one he'd recently begun, but his hair felt so heavy. And before he could stop himself, he was grabbing scissors and standing in front of the mirror again.

Snip. Snip. Snip. No hesitation. His breaths becoming deeper. Snip. Snip. Snip. He was seeing all the events of the past two years. The breakup with Sheron, the clients he felt he failed, his first visit to his mother's grave since he was a child. All those events falling away in dark black locks started after his trip to Jamaica. Falling away. And he was feeling lighter. Snip. Snip. Falling away. After the last lock fell he surveyed himself in the mirror. His hair was short and ragged. He'd get it shaped before work tomorrow. He smiled at himself.

It was only a start, he knew. Things wouldn't change overnight. He was not going to try to make this deeper than it was. It wasn't magic, but it felt good. It felt like magic. He gathered his locks, went to his bedroom and placed the hair in a wooden box he'd bought in Jamaica.

He lay down on his bed. He had to get up early. What a strange night. Suddenly he remembered his promise to Treasure. He took the journal from the table where he'd left it earlier and opened it. On the inside cover was Treasure's purple calligraphy:

> *Tears unshed turn to poison in the ducts.*
> —*Alice Walker*

Dante wrote the date: August 14. Under it he wrote: Happy Birthday, Mom.

It had been a strange night. Then he felt that shifting inside of him again. He started blinking hard. He saw it all. He was a grown black man hurting. He was feeling the stings, but unlike the last time, he was in the privacy of his own bedroom. Dante closed his journal, took a deep breath, and for the first time in a long time he gave himself permission to cry.

Chapter Nine
Sour and Sweet

O ver the next few days, he dialed the number of almost every woman he knew who was still speaking to him, hoping to chase away the emptiness with sweet conversation, a warm body if he could arrange it. He managed a rendezvous or two, but sex just seemed to feed the emptiness, causing it to spread like some ravenous parasite that threatened to devour him from the inside out unless he could figure out how to stop it.

He thought about calling Malik, but wasn't up to the volleying about sexual conquests that would inevitably result. As a last resort, he turned to poetry, wanting to curl up in words, hoping that they would bring him the clarity and understanding he sought.

That afternoon, Dante had grabbed his notebook and just started walking, letting his intuition guide him. After several hours, he decided to stop at a café for tea. Studying the pastry display next to the espresso bar, he felt someone behind him.

"Dante?"

Hearing her voice, he suddenly felt as though his entire body had been submerged in warm water. The noise of the café—the din of conversation and music, the hissing of steam from the espresso machine, the clinking of glasses—began to fade as it, too, was engulfed in the wave of memory that had rapidly invaded and conquered his senses.

"Dante? Is that you?"

The air around him was so heavy he could barely move, barely breathe. It took all the strength he could muster to turn around and face her. But once he did, the heaviness fell away, his lungs filled with air. Her face, as familiar and mysterious to him as his grandmother's house, welcomed him once again. With his eyes, he traced every rise and curve his fingers itched to touch. Her golden skin, the color of wheat. Her cheeks, dotted with small brown freckles, a constellation of stars he had once named before christening each one with a kiss.

"Dante, I'm so glad to see you," she said stepping forward to hug him.

"You, too, uh … "

"Eva. My name is Eva, remember?" Her voice drooped with disappointment as her arms fell back to her side.

"I know that. You think I would forget?" Dante reached for her and pulled her into an awkward embrace. They retreated from one another quickly, as silence rushed to fill the space between them.

"So what are you doing here? I mean, when did you get back from Jamaica?" Dante asked, hesitantly.

"A few months ago, I—"

"You two wanna order something?" the magenta-haired woman at the register interrupted.

"You got time for tea?" Dante asked Eva.

"Sure."

"Jasmine?" he asked. Eva nodded. Dante placed their orders and paid the cashier. They walked down to the end of the counter to wait for their drinks. Eva twirled a cinnamon-colored lock around her finger as she studied the John Coltrane poster hanging on the wall behind the counter. Dante watched her, surprised to find himself still excited by the light citrus scent of her perfume, the soft plumpness of her body. And those eyes, almond-shaped and so brown they were almost black. He could swim in the darkness of her eyes. Eva caught his glance and looked away again.

"Your hair; it's longer," Dante remarked, touching one of her locks. "Last time I saw you, it was just below your ear, now it's almost to your chin."

"That's the amazing thing about hair," said Eva smiling mischievously. "It grows."

"I see you haven't lost that razor-sharp wit," Dante teased. Eva rolled her eyes and mock-punched him on the arm. "Whoa, you're resorting to violence now?" He raised his arms as if to shield himself. "Violence is never the answer," he said, peering through his fingers now covering his face.

"Sometimes it is. Besides, you know you like it rough," Eva's voice dropped to a seductive whisper.

"You remember," Dante said, words opening like doors, wide with possibility. "You remember honey?" he asked, trying to ease the conversation forward.

"Do *you* remember honey?" Eva countered, eyebrows raised. How could he forget? "Honey," as they called it, had been one of their special rituals when they were together. She would paint his body with honey from top to bottom, then lick it all off from bottom to top. And right before she got to his lips, the first and the last place she anointed with her sweetness, she would squeeze a few drops of limejuice onto the tip of her tongue. When she kissed him, his mouth was flooded with sour and sweet. He had started to crave that taste after awhile, started to crave her. Honey was where the trouble began.

Dante pushed the past out of his mind. They were both here now, and the space between them was getting smaller. She still wanted him, he could sense that, despite what had happened between them. He had turned himself into a ghost, pulling away piece by piece until he was completely empty inside, and his body simply followed suit. He had disappeared. A woman's capacity to forgive was an amazing thing, he thought.

"Tea for two." The magenta-haired woman slid a tray with two small ceramic teapots and two empty mugs across the counter. "Let the tea steep a minute more, and be careful, the pots are hot," she cautioned as though giving them parting instructions before they embarked on a dangerous mission.

"Um, could you make mine to go?" Eva asked.

"I thought we were going to sit for a minute," Dante said, disgusted by the pleading tone he detected in his voice.

"I wish I could, but the drinks took so long and now I'm late," Eva shrugged her shoulders.

"How about dinner tonight?" Dante offered. Eva paused to consider the proposition.

"I … well … okay," she said finally, still looking uncertain of her decision.

"Why don't we meet at Zena's at eight?" he prompted.

Eva nodded. She grabbed her tea and blew out of the café with a wave.

* * *

"I saw her," Dante said as soon as Malik picked up the phone.

"Who?"

"Eva," Dante flopped back onto his bed.

"Who?"

"Eva. You know, the girl I met in Jamaica."

"Oh, yeah. Love-of-your-life Eva. The one you ditched for the bikini babe."

"I didn't ditch her for the bikini babe. What was that girl's name? Anyway, I was young and stupid."

"A year ago, right?" Malik chuckled. "You succumbed to the power of the teats."

"That, too. But seriously man, Eva was looking good. And it wasn't just how she looked. The way I felt about her when we were together, it hadn't changed," Dante rubbed his temples with his free hand. "Man, I fucked up," he groaned.

"Hold on a second, I have to get my bearings. I'm being teleported into a scene from *Love Jones*," Malik teased.

"Man, I'm serious."

"Okay, okay. How did it go when you saw her?"

"I don't know. It was kinda awkward at first. But then things started getting cool and she bounced."

"Can you blame her? I mean, sister was into you in Jamaica. She was down, capital D. But you dropped the ball. You were out, man."

"I know, don't remind me," Dante groaned again and curled into a fetal position.

"Karma is nothing to fuck with. But never fear my friend, there's always another chance to show that we've learned our lesson. Another unwitting, innocent soul will come along, they always do."

"Thanks for your kind words," Dante said sarcastically, then sat up abruptly. "You think it's too late with Eva? I'm supposed to see her tonight."

"It ain't over 'til it's over. Which, by the way, this conversation is. I gotta go to work. Some of us actually do work for a living."

"Whatever, man. I'm just taking the day off to clear my head."

"Yeah? Well, keep me posted," Malik said and hung up.

Dante jumped up and started to pace, suddenly filled with nervous energy. What had happened with Eva? Why had he run from her? He remembered the first time they met. It was about a year ago. He had been one of fifty young writers from around the world selected to participate in a two-month writer's workshop in Negril. His being chosen was one of his greatest honors. He had concocted an almost embarrassing web of lies and diversions to get out of work for that long, but it was worth it.

When he arrived in Negril, instead of feeling elated, he felt humble and scared. What was he doing here anyway? Did he have anything worthwhile to say? What if his writing was shit compared to everybody else's? These thoughts were on repeat, looping through his head as he stumbled into the lobby of the hotel where he would be staying. The place was swarming with writers. Different accents, languages, scents and colors swirled around him. Overwhelmed, he dropped everything he had been carrying and stopped in the middle of the cavernous room, his eyes searching frantically for the American flag.

"You look a little lost, can I help you?" A woman's gentle voice broke through the chaos, engulfing him in a circle of warmth and calm.

"I, uh, need to check in. They said to look for the flag," Dante rummaged around in his pockets, looking for his acceptance letter.

"Don't worry about it. I can help you." She touched his arm lightly. "I'm Eva, one of the program assistants. What's your name?" Dante looked at her for the first time. He was transfixed when he met her eyes, they were like two oceans of black water. He just wanted to keep peeling back layers, diving deeper into the darkness. Eva shifted her weight. Dante was embarrassed when he realized that she was waiting for him to answer. He felt himself blush as he gave her his name.

"Oh, yes, Dante. I remember reading your work during the selection process. Really beautiful stuff," she smiled as if nothing had happened and looked him up on her list. She showed him to his room, and later that night, introduced him to some of the other writers and the program directors. The next day, she took him around Negril, divulging the secret spots she'd discovered.

As it turned out, Dante and Eva were from the same city and had many interests in common. They became fast friends. They attended the same workshops and spent hours going over each other's work. They'd call each other up in the middle of the night to share passages from the books they were reading, or to play an excerpt from a song that had moved them. Still, Dante didn't think of Eva romantically. She was like earth, dependable, solid. But there was no spark. Once he started to feel comfortable in his new setting, he began to scope out other women, his attention drawn to the scantily clad beauties he saw almost everywhere he went. He also became infatuated with a performance poet from Chicago, a woman whose energy was like fire.

One night, Eva invited him to her cottage for dinner. They spent the evening chopping vegetables, reading bad poetry aloud and laughing. Dante had never before felt so comfortable with a woman. What would it be like, the two of them together? He was surprised by the thought when it jumped into his head, but then began to consider the possibility.

"Hey, I just had a funny thought," he called out to Eva, who was in the bedroom looking for a CD.

"What's that?" Eva asked from underneath her bed. Before Dante could answer, the front door opened and the performance poet stepped into the room dressed in a skimpy bikini top and a tight African print wrap skirt.

"Peace, brother … I'm Journey, Eva's roommate," she extended her hand. Dante was so stunned, it took him a few seconds to remember out how to move his arm to shake her hand. Eva resurfaced moments later. "Hey J, did you meet Dante?" Journey and Dante nodded. "What was your funny thought?" Eva turned to Dante.

"Nothing," he answered, his thoughts about Eva consumed by the heat of Journey's presence. The three of them spent the rest of the evening together. Journey and Dante passed looks and small touches back and forth. At the end of the night, Journey walked Dante to the small courtyard outside the cottage. She plucked a leaf off a nearby tree, wrote her number on it and pressed it into his palm.

He called her the next day and the next. Each time, she answered the phone with a flurry of crazy excuses to blow him off. "I'm cleansing my energy right now; I'm meditating; I'm going to the water to listen for the voices of the ancestors." Dante felt physically tired after trying to reach her, but he liked the chase.

He started going to the cottage almost every day. Journey was never home. He and Eva fell into a routine. They would cook dinner together and then walk down to the beach behind the cottage. Out there, the world went on forever, and it was just the two of them and the stars breaking the seamless night.

"You ever hear that jazz standard, 'I Fall in Love Too Easily'?" Eva asked one night and started to hum. Dante nodded, reaching for her hand. They danced in the sand, barefoot, to Eva's humming and the sound of water lapping against the shore. Dante held her close, their heartbeats racing and slowing to match one another's. And suddenly, standing there on solid earth, holding Eva, was the only place he wanted to be. Dante lifted her face to his and kissed her. Eva pulled away after a few moments.

"Do you know who I am?"

"Of course I know who you are."

"I'm not Journey. I'm Eva."

"You are Eva. My friend. My earth. The end and the beginning of my journey."

Dante stayed at the cottage for the first time that night with Eva wrapped in his arms. In the morning, he woke to find her sitting beside him in her robe, two cobalt blue bowls balanced on her lap. One of the bowls contained three limes, the other was half-full of honey.

"What's all this?" Dante asked.

"You'll see," Eva said, drizzling honey over him before he could protest. Eva licked every place on his body that the honey had touched. When she got to his face, she painted his lips with her fingers, squeezed juice from one of the limes onto her tongue and kissed him. Every part of him was screaming with desire. He pulled Eva onto him, then gently rolled over and straddled her, his lips never leaving hers. He could barely get the condom on and enter her before his passion was released. They spent the rest of the day in bed, entangled in sticky sweetness.

There was only a month left of the workshop. Dante and Eva spent as much time together as they could. Dante practically moved into the cottage. He had even caught himself referring to it as "home." But towards the beginning of the last week, something shifted, turned just slightly, and the relationship didn't feel the same. Dante remembered the night it happened. He was standing on the beach, looking up at the light coming from the kitchen where Eva was washing dishes. He could see her through the window, wearing a tam he had bought from the Rastafarians over her short dreads, a tank top and a pair of his shorts. He imagined himself watching her like this for the rest of his life. The thought sent a jolt of panic slicing through him like a blade. The wind changed directions, and he caught the scent of lime, which had seeped into his pores by now, wafting up from his skin. Usually the smell made him feel calm, close to Eva even when she wasn't there. But that night, it made him nauseous. He went inside, gave Eva a quick kiss goodnight and went to bed. It would be the last night he stayed at the cottage, his last night in Eva's bed.

The next morning, he woke up early and left quickly, mumbling something about an early class and a poem he had to write. Eva didn't object, just stared at him, holding her head in her hands like a wilted flower.

Dante kept himself busy with his work. Eva didn't call. He was angry that she didn't even care enough to find out what was going on. But even if she had asked, he wouldn't have known himself how to answer.

The morning of his last night in Negril, Dante found a poem from Eva at his door.

On the beach at night, the trees whisper your name and the sand gathers itself around me, trying to fill the space you left behind. The ocean creeps up to the shore and kisses my toes. I thought the moon would guide him back, I say. Silly, girl, answers the ocean. Who do you think makes the tides rise and fall? What was there one night will be swept away the next. Only a fool would trust the moon.

Dante had wanted to go to her, to tell her she was wrong. Instead he stuffed the poem into his back pocket and went to the poetry festival, the last event of the workshop, where Journey would be reading. He left Negril without saying goodbye to Eva. She had stayed in Jamaica to teach writing at one of the local elementary schools. Dante didn't try to contact her once he got back home.

Sitting in his room now, a year later, Dante prayed that he would be able to mend the wrongs of the past.

* * *

Dante arrived at Zena's half an hour early. He was grateful when the hostess sat him at a table in the back corner of the restaurant. He wanted to curl up in that corner, in the shadows of the dimly lit room. He wrapped his hands around the small glass candleholder, absorbing the warmth from the candle inside. He stared into the flame, searching for words that might touch Eva and soothe her heart's hurting places, words that could explain what had happened between them; words with which he could build a bridge back to the sacred space they had created for one another.

"Hey," Eva's voice interrupted his brooding. Dante stood up clumsily to greet her. They sat down, avoiding one another's eyes. The waiter brought menus and water to the table.

"The grilled tuna salad is great here," Dante offered. Eva nodded without looking up from her menu. They each ordered the tuna when the waiter returned.

"Great minds think alike," Dante said and wanted to kick himself for being so corny. With the menus gone, there was nothing to shield them from each other. The table between them was like a wide, open field dividing their turf. Now or never, Dante thought to himself and ventured a first step.

"So, what are you doing back in the city?"

"I'm teaching writing at one of the city colleges. It's pretty cool, but I miss Jamaica."

"Yeah, me, too." Dante paused for a breath. "Look, I made a mistake."

"What are you talking about?" Eva asked, wanting to make him say it.

"In Jamaica. I made a mistake, with us."

"You made a choice."

"I made the wrong choice. I'm sorry if I hurt you."

"Well, if you didn't want to be with me, you could've told me to my face. After all we shared. We were friends first, Dante."

"It wasn't that."

"Then what was it? It seemed pretty clear that you didn't want me."

"I didn't know how to want anyone."

"You wanted Journey."

"Journey was a myth, an idea. She was never real."

"But I was never enough. Never exciting enough, never beautiful enough."

"You were everything I needed. I was afraid."

"I loved you."

"I loved you, too."

"I opened my heart to you, and you took what you wanted and ran."

"I'm sorry."

"You never called."

"I'm sorry."

"I doubted myself."

"I'm sorry."

"It took me that whole year to heal."

"If I could take all the pain away I would. I love you."

"You don't know me."

"I love you."

Eva let the weight of the words wash over her and settle in the middle of the table. She didn't respond.

"Did you get the poem?" she finally spoke.

"The one in Jamaica? Yeah."

"No, the one I left on your answering machine a few days ago."

"That was you?" Dante almost choked on his water.

"Yes," Eva said, disappointed that he hadn't recognized her.

"But you didn't sound like yourself." Dante remembered the morning he had heard the mysterious message, how his own head was reeling with thoughts of Sheron and the disappointment that still lingered after their break-up; the rejection from the woman he had met in the club the night before.

"I wasn't myself. I had just gotten back in town and I was confused and angry and lonely and still in love and missing you. You know, missing you all this time hurt more than the pain of your actual leaving," Eva said quietly. "But I'm clearer now, calmer."

"Look, Eva," Dante said urgently. "I want to try this again. I've never had these feelings before. Can't we just live in the here and now, and tackle the past one piece at a time together?" Eva stared at him for a long while, as though trying to memorize every detail of his face.

"I can't, Dante." She gathered her things and stood up to leave.

"Wait, please, we haven't even eaten. At least share a meal with me," Dante begged. Eva looked at him, torn between the love she still felt surging through her heart and the memory of his leaving that continued to flash in her head.

"It's too late, Dante," she said and stroked his cheek lightly, needing to touch him one last time before she walked away.

Chapter Ten
On Top of the Game

Aug. 15

I'm trippin'
slippin'
like I'm in a room
small enough to be a cell
can't explain
the tightness I feel
words undone
before I get a chance
to put this big jigsaw puzzle to rest
one foul banana peel under my heel

I'm lost in thought
need a break
too much stinging my brain
dizzy blown out and nobody I can tell
this to …

Aug. 16
Called in for work. Women are off limits. For now. Need to write. Nothing. Clear head. Everything is trying to drown me.

Aug. 18
What's the point in being a hermit when nothing is being accomplished? Can't write one poem. One story. Nothing.

Aug. 19
Thank God for vacation days. I realize that the reason everything has turned to mud is because my priorities are fucked up. I am a writer and I don't write everyday. My writing muscle has turned to gook … the phone rings again. Thinking about quitting my job.

Sept. 5
Tried to write in my other journal but couldn't. This is the first one without lines. I am free to write any way I want. In circles, upside down … and it matters.

Story idea: A kid takes to counting the licks on an ice cream cone but every time he gets halfway through someone or something interrupts him.

Sept. 15
Quit my job. It's done. No turning back. Do or die. I am a writer and I must devote my life to living for it ... not for me, but for the words.

Story idea: A woman leaves a quiet comfortable town. Goes to a land where no one speaks the same language. Everything is scattered. A mess. She stays because she is comforted in the fact that the chaos is no longer just inside her.

Sept. 23
Wrote twenty-five pages today. I feel good ... fifteen pages yesterday ... just finished reading *Invisible Man* again ... yeah, I'm on a roll.

Sept. 26
I'm making a pilgrimage to find my soul. Malik called. Can't talk to anybody familiar. Sleeping all day. Up all night has put me right. Twenty-five pages ... not necessarily in the order that the book will be—just this kid's voice talking to me about living in the suburbs and visiting his cousins living in the projects for a summer. This is outside of my life ... tapped into someone else's story. I feel freer now than I ever have.

Oct. 1
Last night my feet rested under a bar with no face. A woman also without a familiar face sat next to me. She asked for a light, which I didn't have, and began to talk. I talked back but the words were empty. They meant nothing ... far enough away to say we were not going to be, but I still wanted her. She knew. Loneliness in both of our eyes, she accepted our fate. Asked me

to touch her chest. Her heart beat like it was in my hand. Her kisses drained me, yet I still had the energy to take. To posses her ... possessed her until she called out the name that had brought her to me. Niles. Her tears stained my shoulder, her nails dug into my skin as if she had buried him there.

It was after that she asked me to tell her my name. Carl. She nodded, knew I was lying. When I left, she said thank you. No words from me but I am grateful for this faceless woman. I realize that I don't just take from women. They need me, too. How many men would feel comforted by a woman calling out another brotha's name?

Oct. 2
Treasure wrote me. Brazil has done a number on her. She's enchanted. Talks about everything from the varying degrees of what the ocean smells like to the millions of colors in a one-block radius.

Oct. 3
So much goin' on ... a month ago I felt like I was standing at the edge of the world and the universe was begging me to jump and now ... this morning gives me sun, the sun gives me a chance to see the world with new eyes ... I've admitted my need for women. As much as I fear them, I realize it is through them I am able to feel. So fuck it. I'm clear. No matter what anyone says this is who I am and with this, at least if I'm honest, I can only be so much of an asshole ... besides I've created my own tormenting demon ... the dog nightmares that make me question my sanity. But if that's the price I must pay to be closer to grace, so be it.

* * *

After they had fucked—not immediately—but soon afterwards, Dante got up looking for his boxer shorts and the rest of his gear. She watched him. Still, silent room. Dark.

"So ... Carl ..."

"That's not my real name."

"I knew that. It's a good name though. It's something very Yin/Yang about it."

"Really?" He tried to sound indifferent.

"Mm-huh, very masculine and feminine." She reached to touch his shoulder as he leaned across the bed searching for a sock or pants. "So Carl ... guess it would be stupid to ask you to stay the night."

"It was stupid of me to come here again." Dante looked over at her. His words laced with a coldness he hoped would fend off any attachment. Continued to put on his clothes.

She rubbed her shaved head, sat up to watch his silhouetted body. "I keep trying to pull my hands through hair that's not there anymore."

Dante was silent. Distant. But his movements weren't as fast. As if he was trying to linger to hear her voice.

"But I like it. I kept feeling that I *was* my hair. Now, I know if somebody is interested in me—"

"I'm not interested."

He went for cruel and won. She nodded. Her face blank. He tried to read her but fell short. Only her voice gave clues to who she was. The voice he didn't want to hear. Shoes on, he sat at the edge of the bed riddled with guilt.

"That was foul ... I didn't mean it like that."

"I know … it's cool … I mean, when I saw you walk in tonight I thought hard about leaving … really had to fight myself to stay. Then I figured that destiny brought us together … I mean, two weeks to the day … not even the same bar."

Dante nodded. He stared long and hard at this woman who had found a way to get to him. Her shaved head took beauty by the throat … defiant. Her skin glowed. Her eyes huge and illuminated. Her fingers as if each one were prima ballerinas, contrasted with a body that had a bit more flesh than he normally enjoyed. Throughout their sex-fest, Dante found himself touching, caressing every bit … wanting more, even when he laid out, exhausted. She was complete in her woman ways. Dante tried to hold her essence. Hoping he could walk away with enough of her fuel to carry him through. He kept staring, trying to get at the something pulling him on an invisible leash. He kept staring, trying to figure out what it was about her that made him want to hurt her and then kiss her wounds caused by his sword tongue. He kept staring.

The pain behind his eyes made her smile, knowing that her hurt mirrored his.

Dante reached, touching one of her legs wrapped in the crumpled sheet, "I gotta go. Next time … if it is a next time … do what you thought about doing."

"I'd like to think I'm that strong."

Dante got up, headed to the door. Never looked back.

* * *

"Wow, you really have journeyed," Malik said to Dante. They sat at the near-empty bar. A basketball game droned in the background. "You look like shit but you sound good," he continued.

"See, normally I would've said fuck you, but I take that as a compliment 'cause I know it's comin' from something you can't help ... bourgie-ass."

"Fuck you."

Malik's "just kidding" grin didn't hide the disdain in his eyes. Something about this new Dante scared him. He knew that they had drifted apart. Knew they would never be as close as they had been. This was the Dante he suspected lurked beneath mortal wounds. Malik knew that if Dante ever reached deep enough into himself to just accept himself as is—without guilt—they would never be tight like they had always been. That day was this day.

"Give me some news about you." Dante's voice was calm and caring.

"Still big game huntin' ... gotta have it." Malik's voice went louder, took to the street as if he was trying to cover a lie with a lie. He smiled at Dante.

"Are you growing from it? I mean, all these encounters?"

"Pussy don't make me grow, man. Just like you were sayin' writing is a muscle and you realize that you need to exercise it? That's what pussy is ... I gotta exercise that shit."

"So going at it just like that ... I mean, it's not boring?"

Malik shrugged, wanting now to disrupt Dante's flow. Wanting to do something to make Dante appear less on top of his game. Malik gulped gin as if the scorch would erase destruction.

"So, you ain't say how you gonna make it without a job."

"I'm straight ... ain't thinkin' about nothing but finishin' this book."

"Can't live on unemployment for long."

"I'm covered, B."

Malik remembered the insurance policies. Dante was covered; his parents had made sure that if something happened to them Dante would be okay. Malik ordered another drink though he had not yet finished the one in front of him.

"So no looking back?" Malik asked. "All past shit is past, huh?"

"Yeah, nothing exists outside of my writing … not even me."

"Hear that. So here's to Dante as writer."

They clinked glasses. Malik downed the last corner of his first drink, made a scowl face.

"Yeah, I was tellin' Sheron a while back that the *real* you was removed from anything."

"I wouldn't say that—"

"Naw, I just meant that, you know … she was feelin' guilty about bein' over my house—"

"Sheron was at your house?"

"At it. In it. Wit' it. Yeah-yeah, son. Mmm-hmm, yeah. It was a while back. She was feelin' guilty, but I said you ain't that kind of brotha to care about shit like that."

Dante's eyes blurred. A trickle of sweat slid down his heated brow. He bit his lip hard enough to draw blood.

"Yeah, a'ight."

"You're not mad or nothing, right?" Malik asked him.

"Naw. Can't be mad at an ass who's just that."

"Yeah, I ain't never lied about who I was. She was sweet too."

Dante's stomach tightened. He knew if he stayed longer he would haul off and punch Malik in his smug face.

"You talk to Lo recently?"

Malik swallowed. The name conjured up a past that he and Dante had made an unspoken pact to forget.

"That's a name out the blue."

"Not at all." Dante raised up, went into his pocket.

"I got this, dog," said Malik.

"Naw, man, I got this one." Dante pulled out a twenty dollar bill and placed it on the warm wood. Disappeared into the night. Malik nursed his second drink. Knew that his words had just cost him his best friend.

* * *

Oct. 25

Rethinking everything. I had accepted my plight to love women on my anonymous level and now I want more than that. Can't commit to one idea … where to go? Rambling down the same streets. Redundacy is boring. Here I am … Malik with Sheron? I can't get it outta my head. It's fucking me up. I thought I would be able to handle some illness like this. And he did it on purpose. If I punched him, if I had … keep writing, write faster get the thought outta my head … what else? Write faster … write to erase … what to say? Talk about new books. Yes! Books I've read this past year … like *Naked Lunch, Negrophobia*, what else? Reread *The Color Purple* … what else? Miles autobiography, what else? I can't believe he fucked her … I need to talk to her … will I be going back in time if I ask her? If I saw her? Am I torturing myself? Why would Malik tell me some shit like that? Gotta let it go … I can't hold on to something that means … what does it mean? I've slowed down, can't write fast because the picture of them can't be erased … can't think of anything but them together … yes, I admit it … how could I have made myself see her only with me? Even though I know what she does for a living, I've seen how she makes men feel, but Malik? Man, if he would do that … where can I place this?

Nov. 1
Another postcard from Treasure. She's decided to stay longer. Thinking about visiting her. But, no. I can't. I have to get strong in what I'm doing. I can't see her unless I'm on top of my game like she is.

Nov. 20
Another bar. Another girl. Another fuck. Empty. I wish it had been her with the shaved head. Baldy.

Nov. 21
Chased my nightmares down. The dogs trying to devour my flesh have become winged animals and I ride them across a sky of sand and ocean. I'm riding them … I've killed the part that makes them ferocious to me and still … I don't ride them in strength and pride but in terror and hopelessness. Today I missed my mother to the point of … I'm tired. I'm stuck. My writing has collapsed. I can't hold any thoughts together. I'm driving myself crazy … images of me being a caught elk under a lion's fangs. Connect to something and there it is: my writing. It saves me and then does it really?

Nov. 23
Frozen. I wish that I had never met up with Malik. I was on a roll. I had figured out a system that was working for me. I was writing. I had come clean. I was at a good place! I was at a real

good place … my best friend? I will have to face him soon but not now, when I blow the fuck up! Eat my dust, bitch. Naw, stop. I want to be at a place where I can only see him as the friend who has been there with me through crisis. Malik the savior … that night he didn't look much like a savior. Over thinking? Was Malik going for blood? I can't help but to think that he was. But why? 'Cause of the questions I asked him? But I was asking more for me! He should've been happy that I was finally figuring my own shit out. No help from him, or Sheron or anybody. But he wasn't. Told me some shit that broke so many of our pacts. #1, Don't fuck anybody the other was ever in love with. #2, If you do #1, don't tell. Never tell.

Nov. 26

Today I went to visit my parent's gravesite. Something I've never done. Sheron had suggested it a while ago. As much as I fight the desire to hate her for what she did with Malik I can only see her as an angel. Treasure, Eva … I see them all as angels. That's what I told mamma … I know that in each of the women that I've connected with is a part of mamma. I talked to daddy too. Told him I wish he was around now to tell me about the dirt a friend can throw; like an old, evil bitch. We could swap stories. Laugh about it all. That's it! This is all a big, fat joke and I'm allowing it to be something more. This shit is funny … I mean, my best friend tells me he fucked my girl? Even though Sheron and I never claimed exclusivity, Malik knew what was up. Rubs it in my face! Daddy would have to laugh. He would tell me … what would he say? Yeah, daddy would've told me to go and kick Malik's ass just for the sake that he must have wanted a beat down. Mamma would say, just let it go … would she though, or would it be the other way around?

Dec. 1

Have had three dreams about that baldheaded girl — correction: woman. She is a woman. Lotta pain. I saw that shit. But still she hasn't let it get to her … I mean, she don't hate men.

Dec. 4

I've built this baldheaded woman a pedestal. Placed her on it. And now I'm on bended knee at her feet. Man, what an asshole … wanting what I don't want. The shit I fuck up. I know why I do this … comes down to my need to feel. Feel something. That's why Malik did that shit to me … 'cause he thought I wasn't feeling anymore … really? Do I really believe that shit? Wow, I'm trying to forgive a brotha who tried to kill me while we threw back a few drinks.

Dec. 6

I'm my best tormentor. Went to shaved head's apartment. Waited like a dumb fool from ten at night until midnight. A dumb fool made lucky only by a mild winter night. She never came home. Then I went back to the two bars … nothing. And I looked in the mirror when I got home to see if my true fool self could be seen. What a mask I have. Well, at least I'm writing again!

* * *

He finally saw her. A crazy red wig on her head that neared her calves in length, a politician's wife tweed suit, and a buttoned fitted multicolored parka made her look like a nut job.

She called out his fake name as he walked out of the post office one block from her apartment.

"You look like you were in a circus," he blurted out before he had a chance to edit his words.

"Yeah, it's my gotta get a job look." Unfazed by his strange stare, she pulled off the red thing clinging to her head.

Dante thought about running. Thought, "Is this the woman I've been idolizing over?" He just stood there waiting, like a tree waiting for the seasons to change.

She brushed the wig, "I went to a few temp jobs without Shirley—that's what I call this one—nothing. They wouldn't send me out. So I got this heifer and now I'm a workin' girl again." She balled it up and stuffed it in her oversized bag.

Dante tried to figure out how to get out but the more she talked the more he wanted her to say more.

"So you've always done your mailing here?" she asked him.

"Yeah … mean, no. I don't go much and—"

"This one is pretty good. The lines are usually short and they play good music."

"Yeah?"

She took a pause to give him the third eye. Smiled after she figured his whole thing. She sized him up so well that she wondered which way to play it. Should she go for the coy? See if he would say his mind. Or should she go straight, no chaser?

Dante began to look goofier as the seconds ticked off. The sweat began to bead up on his nose and then she knew.

"You know, Carl, it can be a zipless fuck. We don't have to ever know each other."

"What?" Dante's voice screeched like he had lost the bass.

"Yeah. You know, we both agree that it's no strings attached. We don't reveal who we are."

"Zipless fuck, huh?"

"It was in a book I read—*Fear of Flying*. It's been a while so I don't remember everything, but the main character was a woman who wanted to have uncommitted sex. She was married but she wanted the intimacy but not the baggage. Did you see *Last Tango in Paris*?"

"No, is that another zipless fuck?" He enjoyed saying these words together.

"I have it upstairs."

A long pause. It was now his move. He didn't want to be cruel, but he really didn't know what he wanted.

"I'm messed up and I don't wanna put—"

"I can't hear this. We're all messed up. I just wanna know who Carl is … and that can be whoever we want it to be. I'm … I dunno, why don't you give me a name?"

"Light? Cloud? I dunno, Sky?"

"Cool, I'm LightCloudSky and you're Carl and whoever else we are won't matter. Okay?"

"Yeah, okay."

Dante followed her into her apartment, heart racing for what he hoped was to be the biggest adventure of his life.

Chapter Eleven
C'est La Vie

"**Y**ou've gotta be kidding." Dante didn't mean to say it out loud. But he did. He also didn't mean to be talking to a door. But he was.

He was talking to the front door of LightCloudSky's apartment building. There was no one else to hear him because it was three fifteen in the morning and he was standing there alone.

* * *

It had still been light outside when Dante first followed Sky into her apartment. The specter of her private space stripped of the nighttime shadows that usually cloaked it in seductive mystery unnerved him. He felt like he was sprawled naked within the probing, circular burn of a spotlight. He avoided touching anything — inexplicably fearful that every texture and surface in her apartment was reaching out for him, trying to capture a small piece of his aura to hold hostage and use to blackmail him into returning and returning and returning again to this bare, single-room home of the baldheaded woman offering zipless fucks.

Thankfully, there wasn't much to touch. A second-hand futon freckled with sporadic red slashes and accidental drips of bright paint jutted out from a wall. It was surrounded by mountains of cardboard boxes so well worn that their paper-thin edges were almost transparent. Each box spilled over with colorful hardcover books that spoke of a range broader than his own. Arcane to contemporary. Fiction to non. Chaste to erotic. Children's books. Occult. Political analysis.

The walls had been painted bright, garish colors and were festooned with objects both interesting and fearsome. Things you might want to touch just to know how they felt, but scary enough not to risk it. He found himself thinking he'd feel safer if each of her walls was enclosed in a glass case.

A phone cord meandered through the middle of the floor like a translucent snake, but it began and ended in Dante's sight and there was nothing attached to either end of it. No phone. No wall jack.

The enigmas multiplied.

No TV. No alarm clock. No doors, except the one he'd just eased through and the one that led to her bathroom. He found himself wondering where she put her clothes. It was an idle thought, but her place was so small that he expected to see at least some sign of them. A shoe peeking out from behind a box, or a coat folded in on itself in the corner. Nothing. There was no hint of a hiding place for the exotic, retro-funky duds she favored. Nothing, except the more formal getup that was currently struggling to hold her curves in check.

He aborted his search for clothing as the windows pulled his attention. They were massive, unfettered by anything except a multicolored puddle of half-melted candles with tendrils frozen in a perpetual drizzle from the windowsill to the floor. Spatters of color blanketed the floorboards in a waxen quilt of rainbows. Outside, some of her neighbors' windows faced hers and Dante imagined there were a few who took delight in watching the life of the strange bald woman who surely wouldn't care if they watched.

He wondered if they'd watched him the last time he was there. He wondered if they'd watched him squirming and pumping above her. He wondered if she'd watched them, watching him. And if she liked it.

Watched … watch … the word called out to him. Lingered in his thoughts until he figured out why.

Oh, yeah. *Last Tango In Paris*. They were supposed to be watching that—isn't that what she'd said? But there was no TV. No VCR. He looked at her. She was balancing on the edge of the futon, drinking him in, warily watching him explore her space. The multicolored parka she'd tossed on the corner of the futon behind her was making a bright batch of color that both contrasted and mixed with the hues of her skin. The tweed suit looked more like rayon now that the light had shifted, but he hadn't seen her dressed for work before. The difference thrilled him. Slightly. He wondered what color would peek out at him if he unbuttoned her top.

Dante licked his lips, setting himself to point out her movie deception, then decided it didn't matter. It wasn't about movies. It was about sex. Zipless sex. And he'd lied too. He'd seen *Tango* before. Many times. He owned it. And he trotted it out like an old, familiar trick every time a sister whose curves he wanted to see silhouetted against his black satin sheets so much as grazed his couch.

Still standing, he asked for a drink and although it was early in the day she read his meaning—made him vodka and orange juice without uttering a word. She watched him as he guzzled it, then made him another. Still silent.

Dante was two sips into the second drink when the liquor finally caught up with his anxiety and before he even realized he'd moved, he was lying in her lap with his head cradled in her arms like a baby. When his defenses had fully wilted against the fresh tide of prickly warm liquor, she spoke. Up close, her voice was like honey drizzled over white-hot charcoal. She could have lured him to the edge of longing like a small pup on a taut leash. He hadn't noticed that before. Or maybe that was the vodka talking.

No. It was her voice. Definitely.

Honey. Charcoal.

She'd said something, but what she'd said hadn't made sense so it didn't stick. He pulled his eyes back into focus. Angled his vision up past the full, rounded push of her chest and sought out the glimmer of her dark eyes. "Hunh?"

"Do you like blondes?" she repeated. He didn't answer because he thought it was a joke. He waited for the punch line.

"'Cause I can be a blonde for you."

136

Oh. So she liked to play rough. Or maybe that was payback for telling her he wasn't interested in her or her bald head only to hunt her down like a scavenger searching for discarded scraps of meat. The comment could have been sincere—some brief glimpse into the treasure chest of pleasures that she was willing to open wide for his erotic satisfaction—but he didn't think so. It stung him as a barely veiled implication that he tended toward white women. Or maybe black women with no backbone. Instantly, he ran with it, inventing new ways that she could have been insulting him and getting angrier with each imagined infraction.

He tensed. Opened his mouth to say something brutal about the night she'd screamed that other brother's name, but she was waiting for it. As soon as he parted his lips she smothered his first two consonants with an engulfing kiss—swallowing his rage whole with the swell of her lips and the softness of her tongue. The Yin/Yang of his bubbling rage in contrast to her lapping kiss made the affection intense. Ushered him toward ecstasy. The winter swirling inside him melted bit by bit as she sucked the anger off his tongue and let it dribble into the softness of her mouth.

Overtaken by her power, he reached up for her, and in response she sent her fingers dancing out in individual explorations of his body. One set twirled pirouettes over the features of his face and shimmied into the tangled knot of his coarse hair like it was made of the familiar twigs of her own nest. Made him feel snuggled. Safe. The other set of dancing digits had more devious designs. They strode purposefully across his torso in a sultry tango, before lindy-hopping in a brief, teasing jaunt down his thigh, and finally stalking back up to meet the hardness uncoiling in his pants with a *muy calienté* salsa.

She cut to the chase, manipulating him firmly and evenly through the dark denim of his jeans until he shuddered helplessly deep into her lap while she hugged him tightly against his shivers. His body vibrated itself into a glassy stupor that almost shattered when he opened his eyes, but she swept them closed again with her ballerina fingers. He tried to fight back but the weight was already pouring into his body like quickly sifting grains of lead. The second time she brushed his eyes closed, he gave in, allowing the powerful release and the burn of vodka to wash him instantly into a deep, fulfilling sleep.

* * *

When he awoke, he was groggy but satiated. His hips seemed to hover just above the futon in an invisible bubble of helium-filled bliss. He lay still in her lap, letting his eyes adjust to the darkness and listening to her hum a repeating refrain from a blusey jazz tune he didn't recognize.

Wait. It was dark. He'd slumbered into the evening and yet she was still sitting beneath him. Still. With nothing to entertain her but her own internal music and the lumbering rhythm of his sleeping breath. She'd just let him sleep. Until it got dark. And she hadn't moved.

He tried to brush it off—tried to not to find the gesture endearing, but he failed. Instead, he found himself stretching out a cautious finger for her lips. She felt him stir and looked his way. Saw his upraised hand and inclined herself to meet it while the roundness of her bare head cast an ebony silhouette against the ceiling. Her lips yielded to his touch like twin sticks of freshly warmed butter.

"Better?" She slid the word out past his finger in a soft puff of warm air. He withdrew his hand quickly, wanting to pretend that her single word question hadn't made reference to the discomfort he'd exhibited earlier. He wanted to think that he wasn't so transparent. He wanted to believe her a less altruistic person than one who would pleasure him just to take the edge off his mood. That kind of giving could ensnare him like the gossamer threads of a black widow's web. So he didn't answer her. But she knew he wouldn't, and had already moved on to other topics.

They talked. Feeling more playful after a bit, his fake name morphed from the simple Carl to the more exotic Carlton Alizé Bedrock, but he threatened to spank her with a paddle if she ever called him anything but Colt .45. She grinned, called him Mr. Sambuca and dared him to do something about it. Then she played along too, rebirthing LightCloudSky as Sky Mistress Margarita Jonez, "With a Z, not an S, baby." She claimed Sky Jonez was an uptown nanny and Mistress Margarita was her alter ego who did devilish dominatrix duty at a place called Nipple Twists. She said the rich, white man she worked for during the day had come in to Nipple Twists one night and hadn't realized that the tall, bald beauty forcing him to roll naked in banana peels was the same one that cradled and fed his children every day.

They both laughed loudly and when they did, Dante realized it was the first laugh they'd shared. They kept it going, making up lives for themselves that were as fantastic as they were funny.

He told her he was a bedspring squeak reducer who did outcalls only. He'd crawl under each bed and scrub the springs with a Crisco-saturated toothbrush all night. It got tricky when the clients decided it would be kinky to make love with him trapped beneath the bouncing springs. Those were the nights that he came home so scratched up that it looked like he'd been thrown into a litter of stray cats. For a week afterwards he'd have to wear a haphazard collection of gauze and Band-Aids that made him look like a budget knock-off of the invisible man.

She liked that one and tried to best it with a tale of being a roving doorknob disinfector, "'Cause, hey, you never know what the hell your friends have been touching up on." He laughed his way into the bathroom. When he came out, the futon had been unfolded into a bed. They talked some more. But not much.

Things other than talking followed quickly. He steered them away from intercourse. Wanted to see what else she had to offer. See if she was as creative as he thought she might be. Revisit her lips.

It was luscious. He made an effort to give more than he received—she at least deserved that. They slept after. But even as his eyes fell closed he knew he didn't plan to stay.

At two in the morning, he rose to slip out without having to say goodbye. It was fun and there were no visible strings but he felt like her apartment was slowly robbing him of air. His fear of the textures in her house capturing parts of his aura reasserted itself.

He got all the way to the front door of her building before he saw it. Somehow he must have missed it earlier. Probably too focused on not waking Sky up during his stealthy escape. But, now, standing with his hand frozen on the building's front door he couldn't miss it.

"You've gotta be kidding me." He didn't mean to say it out loud. But he did. He also didn't mean to be talking to a door. But he was.

Snow. Buckets of it. It was falling out of the sky by the truckload. He shook his head. The city would shut down. The taxis had surely stopped running by now, and even if he trudged through the snow until he found a train station he didn't know which train it would be. A fact that could prove problematic since he lived in a transportation dead-zone that required a damn wilderness hike from the nearest train. It was a daunting walk in the middle of summer with a curvy woman to keep him company. In the snow, by himself—he didn't even want to think about it.

He was stuck.

"*C'est la vie,*" he muttered to the door with a sigh. Then he shuffled back into Sky's apartment—thankful her front door didn't have an automatic lock—undressed and quietly crept into her bed.

"Thought you left." She surprised him with the awakeness of her voice. There might have been knives lurking in her tone but he wasn't sure.

"Nah," he lied effortlessly. "I was gonna get some juice, but it's snowing."

She didn't answer for so long he thought she'd drifted back to sleep. Then she moved. Looked up at her big windows and the endless white dollops fluttering past.

"They look like butterflies," she said after a while, "white butterflies." And in saying so she made him look through the window with her eyes. He saw what she saw. To him it looked like the butterflies were kissing, but that was more than he felt like sharing.

"Guess we snowed in, Colt .45."

He winced, but managed to keep the distress out of his voice as he mumbled his agreement. Then he asked why all her books were hardcover, more to change the subject than to know.

"Why you wanna know that?" There was no mistaking the edge in her tone. He'd made a misstep of some sort and he thought quickly about how to remove his foot from the landmine without causing himself harm. It wouldn't do to be kicked out in the middle of a snowstorm. Not at all.

"I dunno," he answered quickly, then gave it some thought. "I guess you seem like a traveler. Like you might want to start reading something as you leave, and be done with it by the time you get where you're going. Seems like a little paperback would be better for that."

He was surprised by his answer but he liked it. He nodded his own affirmation even though she had her back to him. If she hadn't been propped up on one elbow he would have thought she was sleeping again. So still. So quiet. The river that runs deep.

Finally, she sat all the way up and cocked her head in his direction. The pinkish glow from the accumulated snow threw a small pool of illumination around one of her smooth eyes. Her gaze cut deeply into his.

"What?" he asked, already trying to estimate how far he'd have to leap to grab his clothes and make it to the front door in one fell swoop. She looked a little longer, then shook her head and re-deposited her eye into the shadows. Her hands came up, groping for the hair that wasn't there, and the sheet fell from her bosom as she did. She was ample and the silky light filtering in through the windows seemed like it was straining to contain her generous curves. He was about to say something when she rolled toward him, her breasts swinging loosely as she did. When her back was nestled close against his chest she gave him her response. The edge in her voice had retreated.

"Guess I don't travel as much as I used to."

A long moment later she said she was cold. He wrapped an arm around her, and she overlaid it with her own before she moved his hand up to cup one of her breasts. She let it rest there long enough for both of them to get used to the warmth of it before she started pressing her hips back against his in a very subtle rhythm. Enticed, he kissed the back of her neck. Gently. She moaned. Softly. A brief escape of air with just a hint of volume. He liked the response so he kissed her again. Harder. A little nibble at the end. She liked that. She told him so.

Honey. Charcoal.

She kept talking and her voice lured him to the edge. He let himself tumble over the side. This time he wanted sex and somehow she knew that too. Though later, he would decide that it was her who had wanted sex, then made him want it … and he'd just made the mistake of thinking it was his idea.

Magically, the smooth foil of a condom wrapper was just there, pressed between his fingers as he pinned her hands above her head—subtle enough for him to ignore it if he didn't want to go there, but direct enough for him not to miss a step if he did.

He didn't miss a step.

And while they wriggled themselves against each other and struggled to contain the low guttural sounds that curled through their throats, they both kept their eyes open to watch the white butterflies kissing outside her windows.

Dec. 10

Spent the whole weekend snowed in with Sky. Too much time. Too little to do besides the obvious. Wanted to leave every couple hours, but the snow held me captive. And each minute I stayed I could feel her power twirling icy cartwheels deeper into the joints of my bones. It's crazy, but I swear she made it snow just to keep me there. Thinking of her makes me think of crack pipes. The crack feels good when you're smoking it, but ya gotta know it's gonna mess you up later. Ya gotta know. I dunno ... I just feel bad vibes hovering on the periphery of this self-inflicted bliss. She's trouble. My own personal crack pipe. She asked me for my number. Said she would give me hers but she didn't have a phone. I wanted to say, "No shit." I told her I'd turned mine off so I could focus. She knew I was lying but she pressed me anyway, "Focus on what?" Bed springs, I said, and she smiled. A mask of humor hiding pain. Malik is still right here. Pressed harshly into the corners of my mind. My zipless weekend with Sky wasn't enough to exorcise his demon. I wanna call Sheron, guilt her up with a vengeance. But she can out-argue me and I'd end up feeling like I'd wronged her instead of the other way around.

Dec. 11, 6am

I dreamed of Sky. She had sharply pointed clouds for wings and teeth made of tar. She bit me. I screamed. Her teeth crumbled into a thousand scorching hot raisins that drizzled down my chest and clung, hot and sticky, in my crotch. The phone woke me up before I was burned. No message.

Dec. 12, 8am
I'm leaving. Gotta get out. What did that crazy chick Journey say? Oh yeah, "cleanse my energy." Yep. Gotta go "cleanse my energy, listen for the spirits of my ancestors" and alla that. Don't know where. Can't afford Jamaica.

Dec. 12, noon
Bus Station. Watching the crazies.

Story idea: A corporate recruiter relocates from a big, urban concrete jungle to a small farm town. He's bored silly and finds he actually misses even the discomforts of home. So he starts recruiting local residents to come down to the city's bus station and act like crazies. They get fringe benefits & pay. He gets a comfortable sense of his big city hometown and the city is able to win the well-earned title of "The Capital of Crazy," which would also be the title of the story.

Dec. 12, 5pm
Washington, DC. I'm tired of the baby crying two rows back.

Story idea: A scientist invents an electronic collar that makes white noise at the same decibel level of the person wearing it. So babies can cry soundlessly and women can scream during sex without waking the neighbors. He gets Li'l Kim to endorse it. Makes eight million bucks on the Home Shopping Network. Then goes broke when everyone decides they'd rather hear the screams—to hell with the neighbors.

Dec. 12, 9pm
Richmond. Who on this earth stills wears Brut?? Who besides this flannel-wearing, lumberjack-looking fool next to me? He must be a spy sent to kill me slowly by poisoning my olfactory senses. If I had some CK1 I'd spray him with it. No lie. All over him. No empty seats to move to. Mind over matter. Mind over—awww, fuck it.

The guy behind me is trying to pick up the hottie across the aisle. What is he, deaf? She must have mentioned her boyfriend about ten times. I'm having a hard time resisting the urge to make a big sign that says "No chance, loooooser" and holding it over my seat.

Dec. 12, midnight
Raleigh. Exhausted. Sister at McDonald's gave me some free fries. Ego boost. Can't sleep on bus. Losing focus.

Dec. 13, midnight
West Palm Beach. Good enough. Feeling fuzzy. Need to sleep.

Dec. 14
Just woke up. What the hell?? I don't remember how I ended up at this hotel. Feel like I was in a fugue state and someone else was at the controls. I'm sitting in a suite! On the beach! There is a pool in the living room! No, not a Jacuzzi. A small swimming pool! Inside the room! I must have lost my mind last night. A swimming pool?? Maybe I can get my money back.

I yelled and acted crazy but I can't get my money back. I stopped yelling promptly when he reached under the counter. I ain't stupid. I missed check out time too. Might as well try and enjoy it.

Dec. 14, 3pm
The pool is smaller than I thought. It's about the size of one of my two rooms … okay, that didn't sound right. Never mind — it's big as hell, it's just not Olympic sized. It's heated too. Forgot how much I love to swim. Reminds me of Jamaica all over again. Just what the doctor ordered. Wonder if I can find some ackee and saltfish.

Malik can pucker up and kiss my … peace. Peace. Peace.

Dante sat at the edge of the pool, his feet dangling into the dark, liquid warmth beneath him, and stared at the erratic shimmers of candlelight playing over the water's surface. He kicked a leg and watched the water curl itself slowly into a soft wave, roll away from him, then return in a wide fan of ripples. For the first time in recent memory his mind was quiet. After he'd rimmed the pool with as many candles and sticks of jasmine incense as he could buy, his thoughts had been pried away from him like bricks pulled from loosened mortar.

With his back propped against the cool cinderblocks of the surrounding wall, Dante's eyes fell closed. The candlelight and waves lulled him as sleep cast a fleeting net over his soul.

Sheron. Her hair fell in thin, reddish braids that mirrored the svelte-ness of her figure and swept rhythmically across the tops of her shapely bare breasts. Her eyebrows were pinched into a frown of pleasure, her teeth were creasing the corner of her bottom lip.

"You like that, baby?" Her murmur was all smoke and electricity.

"Oh ... yeah ...," He could barely get it out.

"Yeah? You sure?" Knowing.

"Oh, shit ... yeah ...," Losing control.

"You want some more, daddy?" Knowing he couldn't take it.

The voice beneath her grunted and heaved, swallowing whatever words he'd just formed back into his throat, then he jerked upright as if she'd yanked a pulley that connected to the center of his chest. When his face pulled close to hers she slapped him hard enough to make it sting, then trapped his chin in the vice grip of her palm.

Relishing her moment of control, she talked him up nastily.

"You like it, don't you? Huh? You like that? Say you like it. Say it." He obliged as best he could and she upped the ante. "Is this mine? Huh, baby? Is it mine?" When he finally managed to give her the answer she wanted, his voice cracked and went high.

The talking had excited her, gave her more energy than she thought she had. She channeled it, clutching his head tightly to her bare chest and swaying like a frantic tornado until the bed canted half an inch away from the wall and she forced him to explode between her thighs in a fierce series of swells and ebbs. She slowed down as he twisted and groped wildly at her shoulder blades and the empty air behind her back, then leaned to his ear and coaxed him toward completion with a repeating refrain of "Yeahbaby—yeahbaby," until his groping hands finally settled peacefully around her waist.

She thought it was over. Savored the idea that she had worn him out too badly to reciprocate. But she was wrong.

Slowly, he slid his large hands down to cup and squeeze the heart-shaped cleft at the root of her spine. He caressed her. Rubbed her. Made her feel just the slightest inkling of being turned on again before he shocked her by hauling off and slapping both cheeks of her ass. It was so unexpected that it made her jump. It took her a moment to realize that she'd liked it. A lot.

She was just beginning to hope he'd do it again when his fingers abruptly clamped down deeply into her cheeks and yanked her up along the hard angles of his body with a power she hadn't expected. It startled her, but she liked that too. He didn't even give her a chance to recover. He clutched her up, and pushed her down, clutched and pushed, clutched and pushed, flexing his abs until they wedged up against her, adding extra friction to the spicy mix. She was still sitting above him, but now he was controlling her from below and the contrast thrilled her, brought her to the verge quickly. She fumbled for something to steady herself, finally found the headboard and the back of her own head and seized them both until she found herself brazenly shouting expletives and struggling to ride the spasm of powerful ripples shooting through her body.

Then they held each other tightly and passed aftershocks back and forth like love taps until their bodies became still.

When Sheron finally let go, Dante could see that it was Malik's face that was kissed with sweat beneath her not his own. She sat astride him silently while they settled back into themselves and managed to look everywhere except at each other. Simultaneously, they withdrew, retreated, and came to rest facing opposite directions. Blanketed thickly in shame, neither one of them moved. They lay there wet, quickly becoming sticky, each wishing for sleep to overtake them soon and give them escape from this glaring moment of clarity when their rational minds had overtaken their lust.

Dante's eyes slid open. He thought he'd have to gasp for air or throw up but he didn't. The warm waves still held him, swayed him, kept his mind loose from any high or any low. He let the imagery wash over him, through him, and out of him. And it was done.

He'd let himself see it—how it might have been—and he'd survived. He hadn't slit his wrists or, worse, tried to slit theirs. The lovemaking he saw was desperate and lonely, each of them trying to plug holes that the other couldn't see, and each trying to escape from the other once the act had ripped those holes even wider.

He'd been worried about this moment. The moment when his mind broke through his stockade of defense mechanisms and took him there. He'd been terrified because he'd accumulated too many sexual details about both of them for it to be an easy journey. He knew what Sheron liked, what she did, and what she did extremely well. He knew Malik's twisted ways and the kinky hoops he bragged about making women jump through. He thought it would be too much for him. But he hadn't considered the him-ness that would affect them both. The essence of Dante that would have no choice but to underlie and disrupt their passion. He was there. He had been there. He was certain of it. And even if he hadn't been there, the thought gave him peace.

He lowered himself into the water. Submerged himself into the warm darkness and imagined the water was filtering through his head, rinsing all his painful thoughts and cleansing them. He was far away. In Jamaica. Negril. Swimming naked in the ocean. Someone was cooking him enough bammy and escovich to eat all night. Everything else was a million miles away.

In the morning he was clear. He walked out onto the beach, opened his journal, took a deep pull of the peppermint tea he'd brought from the hotel, and let his fingers blur as they struggled to keep pace with his thoughts.

Dec. 15, noon

With friends like these, who needs enemies?
What's that you always say, Malik? XTP. As in, I XTP'ed her ass. Short for, "X'ed the Toxic Person," ain't it? We been sayin' XTP for so long I forgot how we came up with it. Don't remember your clinical psycho-speak for what a toxic person is supposed to be either, but I got my own definition. Someone who makes you feel bad. Dig that. Just someone who makes you feel bad. You make me feel bad, Malik. All the damn time. I think that's all you've ever done. I come to you when I'm hurt, you beat me down and make me think I need you and your advice just to get by in a world I can't ever hope to survive on my own. I come to you on top of my game and you steal it away from me like it frightens you to see happiness in my possession. Or maybe it threatens you ... but who cares which? The more I think about it, the more all your bullshit comes back to me. Random times you screwed me over just for recreation, like I was your private

151

slot machine that always paid out just when you needed it. I don't even know how we became friends. Wait. I take that back. I guess that was because of Mr. Crisser. Remember him? The old, wrinkled guy with the eye patch and wooden cane. Used to give out candy from the top floor of the tenement we grew up in. You hated him because he didn't like you. You were always complaining about how bad Mr. Crisser would treat you. Cuss you out, chase you away with his cane ... normal grumpy old man stuff, but it bothered the hell out of you—probably 'cause it let you know that there was someone out there in the world that didn't like you, and that was more than your fragile ego could bear. You took it too far when you started seriously plotting to saw his cane just enough so that it fell to pieces when he tried to use it. It bothered me that you wanted to hurt him so much. Maybe he deserved it, but he deserved it from me, not from you. I said so. You asked me why and I shook my head fiercely, trying to shake the memories loose as much as trying to deny you their secrets. You persisted, and somehow I convinced myself that the indignation in your voice meant that you'd have my back. So, I let it out. The secret I'd been holding hostage for two years. I told you about the time I went to Mr. Crisser's place to get some candy. It was hot. Middle of the summer. He asked me in. Said he needed a light bulb changed. Told me he had AC even as I could feel the cool tickles dancing lightly across my face. Said he had ice cream in the fridge. No one was around to go in with me ... but it was hot. Middle of the summer. And we didn't have AC or ice cream in my apartment. I should have waited for someone else. Come back with my mother. I should've. But I didn't. He waited until I got to the top of the ladder before he caressed me. So that if I tried to escape I'd fall and crack my head open on his beige parquet floors. I froze in childhood panic while he slid a leathery hand up the leg of my shorts and worked his scratchy fingers beneath the elastic of my underwear where he caressed and stroked me like a lover. He never stopped talking the whole time. Rambling on with some jilted justification about how what two people decide to do in the privacy of their own home is their own business—as if I was an adult and I'd chosen this encounter. When he slid his tongue over the flesh of my stomach I couldn't hold the whimpers and tears back any longer. The doorbell rang. I think it was the fear of me crying out while someone was standing at the door that finally forced him to let me down. But even then he'd promised to put his glass eye in my food every day if I ever told. I knew my mother's temper would get her thrown in jail if I even hinted at it, so you were the only person I shared the secret with. When I finished, you just stared at me—and from that day to this all you ever said was, "You lying," before you awkwardly changed the subject. You started calling me every day after that, even though I never gave you my number. The next time we hung out with Lo and the whole crew you called me your best friend and, although the rest of the crew couldn't have cared less, no one was more surprised than me. My protest caught in my throat—too polite to challenge you even though I didn't feel the same way. I let you attach yourself and your label to me without wanting either. We were still kids but I should have known then that I would be nothing but a yardstick to measure your own success by my failure. I guess you were a habit I was too nice to break. Like Lo ... until he crossed the line. But everyone has a threshold ... and you just crossed mine. I don't know how I missed it before, but it ain't lost on me now. You know what comes next cuz you made up the phrase. So, XTP, bruh. You been XTP'ed. Step off. It's about time for you to find a fresh punching bag.

Dante's pen stilled. He hadn't even realized he'd forced the memory of Mr. Crisser out of his mind and now that the memory had resurfaced it was wreaking havoc in his head. He measured the memory against his life and found a soul-jarring match. Then he measured it against Malik ...

Measured twice. Cut once. Found nothing.

Dante scoured his memory. What he found was the lunchtime conversation when Malik had hurled "Where you goin' with yo' shit," at him like a fastball full of ice and jagged shards of glass. It had struck him so deeply that the impact hadn't even registered. But it had still done damage. Pushed him towards cliffs and bluffs. Surely there had to be something positive connecting him to Malik—some much more significant glue binding them.

He clawed and scratched at his memory. He came up with nothing.

Dug deeper.

Ripped.

Yanked.

Pleaded.

Still came up with nothing.

Dante held his fists to the side of his head and tried to breathe through his phlegmy rattle of sadness. When he squeezed his eyes shut to end the trickle of liquid pain that was easing from their corners, he saw the cage. The same one Malik had always been able to see. Then he dragged himself back to the hotel with twin trails of salty tears catching every spare grain of sand and pushing the tangy grit into the edge of his mouth.

There was nothing to do but lie on the bed and wait for the emotional drain to pound him into sleep.

Dante's eyes flicked open. His heart was racing but he felt as though he'd been thawed from a glacier, which had held him since the dark ages.

Freer somehow. Uncaged.

He put a hand to his chest. Felt his heart trying to break through his ribcage. Must have had a dream about the dogs again, he thought.

When he'd gotten some more peppermint tea, he re-read what he'd written and waited for more feelings to come. Trying to see if there was any sadness left.

No sadness, only anger. He relived the symphony of minor and major hurts he'd suffered at Malik's hands, all of them still fresh because Dante had never given them voice.

There were too many to write down. They kept popping into his head one after the other like there was a devil's apprentice fiendishly programming pop-ups into his psyche. Each one made him angrier than the last. He found himself mumbling, saying now—to the sand and shells outside his window—what he should have said to Malik previously. Reliving each tortured moment in feverish pitch but handling it the way he wished he had handled it the first time.

He let the feelings rage then, right when they reached their peak, he lit the candles and swam until he was exhausted. The swim evened him out. He dried off and decided he was done with Malik. Time to press on. He ordered room service and let his freshly-delivered plate of sautéed vegetables and rice remain pretty and untouched as he crammed more words into the pages of his journal.

Dec. 15, again

And the trophy goes to …

When I was a boy I realized that sometimes the trophy matters even more than what it was awarded for. Guess you know where I'm going with that, huh? Even in writing it's hard to say … Sheron, you were my trophy. When I first saw you I was vulnerable and you had everything I needed to be swallowed whole: a face that angels would fight over juxtaposed with a body designed for serious sin. You had all the physical specs I always fantasized about—right down to the inch. My perfect physical ideal, come to life. The fact that you were a stripper made it all the sweeter. Even as one of those conscious, Uhuru-type brothers who had written more than a few poems about misogyny and respecting the black woman, seducing a stripper was still a fantasy I couldn't resist. Strippers. The personification of sexuality. Seductive, enticing, so fine you'd pay cash money just to see them put that perfect body close to your face, and able to work their hips so well you couldn't help but wonder what it'd be like to experience those same movements at home, between your sheets—and then shudder at the mere thought of it. Women so comfortable with their sexuality, so uninhibited, that anything could happen. I was trapped from the moment I saw you and all I could do after that was twist and try to squirm myself out of your web. But I wanted to be caught, so it didn't matter. I used everything I had to get to you, to break you down, to make you want me … only to discover that I didn't want you. The fantasy held me close to you for a while. The dream realized of seducing a stripper. But you and I couldn't work. Too many differences that were originally disguised as similarities. Too many fights born out of a soul wounded enough to make exotic dancing your profession. In dealing with you, I dealt with issues I hadn't faced since high school. Evidence of insecurities I thought everyone our age had conquered. Toughed it out because I loved you; or thought I did. But you were always too much for me. Too much. Too much of everything both good and bad. My stuff ain't perfect but I know our individual baggage could never mesh. You were my trophy but now you've fallen from the pedestal and neither one of us has the strength of patience (or bonding) to weld all the pieces of "us" back together again.

Dante looked at what he'd written. As usual, his thoughts surprised him. Whenever he put his pen to paper his feelings poured out of the back of his mind and he discovered things that he never knew he felt glaring up at him in the red ink of his favorite pen.

He looked. Reread his thoughts on Malik and Sheron once more. Stared up at the ceiling and waited for the emotional deluge that must surely follow, but this time it didn't come. He was peaceful, centered, content.

He picked up his red pen again. He was smiling when he made the next entry.

Dec. 15, midnight
I'm back.

Dec. 16
On the bus. I don't even want to talk about how much I had to pay at check out. Clearly I need to quit all this writing nonsense and open a hotel in Florida. It was worth it though. Every penny. I think mamma would approve. You have to pamper

yourself every once in a while and she always used to tell me that peace of mind is priceless. So I'm gonna release my thoughts about the loss of money and focus on the clarity I've gained. I'll say it again. I'm back, baby. Whatever Malik stole from me, I now have in abundance. Bring it on. It's time to blow up.

Dec. 18

> *ain't slippin'*
> *refuse to trip*
> *gore-tex tuff love layered thick on my soul — twice*
> *wrapped tight*
> *ain't lettin' nuttin' outside this flame be tame*
> *my flow, no blow, I know*
> *banana peels be gone*
> *cells be lock-picked*
> *no stix*
> *strength, rhythm, me*
> *begat 6*
> *plus peace*
> *now*
> *floats on 7*
> *—me, myself & I*

* * *

Back in his apartment, Dante didn't even check his messages. He didn't want to know. He just unplugged the answering machine and turned the ringer off. Then he began his writing ritual. He hid all the clocks so he couldn't talk himself out of writing because of the lateness of the hour, angled his computer desk to block the front door so he couldn't even leave his apartment without facing down his urge to write, and left the bathroom light on so he wouldn't forget to take a shower as he stumbled by on his rotating path from bed to computer and back again.

Then he went to sleep.

The calm before the storm.

In the morning he got hype. 50 Cent, Ludacris, Jay-Z. His neighbors must have been pissed, but he didn't care. He topped it off with some old school Mariah Carey. He needed to bring the tempo down and he wanted her "Make It Happen" joint to be the last song he heard before he got into the mix.

If you believe within your soul
just hold on tight and don't let go
you can make it
make it happen

Damn real. Malik would have laughed until tears ran down his face, but Dante didn't have to worry about that any more. With Mariah's words still ringing in his ears he put on the serious shit. Coltrane.

A'ight. Computer on. Fingers poised. Ride or die.

* * *

Two days later the words were coming so fast that Dante had forgotten that he couldn't type. He'd begun by trying to continue the book he was working on when he last saw Malik, but that was dead now. His mind refused to wrap itself around that point of focus. Instead it blossomed and flowered in the realm of his own stories of intimacy, love, and love lost.

He was a banshee. A vampire. A creature of the night who took only brief naps during the day. He ordered in because it took less time than cooking, but then he wouldn't eat what he ordered. Just nibble, drink copious amounts of water and mumble to himself as he tried to figure out the next sentence. He slept, wrote, ate, and paced the floor in the same sweatpants and T-shirt until the smell reminded him to change.

He didn't know where he was going, but he was loving the journey. He had it bad—and it was the best thing that ever happened to him.

Dec. 25

Xmas. Kiss-mass. Kiss-my-ass. The day I gave my parents away to the front fender of a dented pick-up truck with Alabama plates. Ho, ho, ho. The pain is overripe and weighted but I refuse to drown in liquor this year.

Dec. 26

Happy Kwanzaa. Didn't drink. I feel better, but I smell awful. Leaving the bathroom light on obviously didn't work. Raise your hand if you're *not* sure. But lemmie finish this chapter first.

Dec. 27

I'm taking some space from the work. I think I've done what I can do right now. I've got the ideas on paper. I'll go back in a couple days to see what it looks like and clean it up. Right now I need to clean MYSELF up. For real this time.

Dec. 27, again

I'm sharp. Fly. Looking good. Sheron used to accuse me of being scared to be sexy, because I'm always saving my "nice" clothes for later and dressing down. She'd be proud of me today. I'm rocking all my flyest gear even though I'm only going out to get some air and rediscover the world beyond my two rooms.

Ain't smoked a joint since the night Treasure left her panties in my milk carton. Think I'm done with that for good.

A'ight, I'm about to be out. Lemmie get some tangerines from Mr. Hancock's store and start the rest of my day. Yeah, I know they're out of season, but it's tradition.

Dec. 27, 11pm

It don't get weirder than this. First time outside the house and I ran into everyone. A'ight, so maybe not everyone, but enough people to reconnect with the fact that this is my home, these are my peeps, and some of these cats got love for me. Ran into Malik, too. Dig that. He was buying two cups of tea to-go. One of 'em was mandarin orange—Sheron's favorite. Maybe he saw me sitting there, maybe he didn't, but I made sure he saw me before he left. He took a step back when I stood up. Looked wary. Not quite tense but wary, like he wasn't sure what to expect, whether or not he'd have to put down the cups of tea. I asked him if the other cup of tea was for Sheron. The very first words out my mouth. Threw him off something fierce. He finally recovered. Said no. I said too bad, sorry it didn't work out. His jaw tightened. Asked me to go catch a kung-fu flick. His treat. Lame attempt to reassert control. I said, "No." No explanation. No discomfort. No modifiers. Just, "No." I think he left his bottom jaw on the floor of the cafe. I've traveled well. I'm getting more comfortable with me.

Dec. 28
'Bout to get back to this novel soon. I'ma chill until the New Year though. Write poems or something. Stay in the house and just be with me. Oh, I got more postcards from Treasure. Maybe I'll make a collage.

My hair is growing back pretty thick. Think I'm just gonna let be wild this time. Unconfined by the regimented parameters of locks … or anything else. Just like me. The new me. Dammit.

Dec. 28, late
For Sky Mistress Margarita Jonez—

> *We wear the mask that grins and lies,*
> *It hides our cheeks and shades our eyes …*
> *—Paul Laurence Dunbar*

But with us there is no discovery—only falsehoods and wishes for people past. No reality. Only fantasy.

(Oh, snap. Didn't know Dunbar was still in me. Wonder who else is in here. Maybe I'm deeper than I thought).

For Treasure—
So I guess you kept your word. You saved me. Twice. I thought your gift of a journal was simple and silly, but in the end it gave me all the berth I needed to carve myself into who I am. Who I need to be. I should have known better. Nothing with you is

ever as it seems. Those beads you wear signify something, don't they? They must. I guess I knew that already. Thank you, Treasure. When you return to me I will respect you as the teacher you've become. And I never answered you but, yes, you can dance at my wedding. I'd be honored.

For Eva—
I owe you a poem. But I want to share one with you that I didn't write.

> *Seems lak to me de stars don't shine so bright*
> *seems lak to me de sun done lost its light*
> *seems like to me der's nothin' goin' right*
> *sence you went away.*
> *—James Weldon Johnson*

I miss you because I recognize that I loved you. It was the wrong time or I was just the wrong person—not because it wasn't supposed to be *me*, but because I wasn't yet the me that I am supposed to be. I miss you. Thank you for giving me "honey" and for loving me … despite myself.

A haiku for Eliza—

> *Me, moved in soft waves*
> *Hardened by edges of you*
> *Seek not destiny*

Dec. 29, morning
The dogs came back last night. They started to attack but couldn't reach me, then they turned into buzzards and other

flying beasts and tried again, still to no avail. I was at the top of a mountain. I ran down the side of it holding a white silk sheet that ballooned and carried me into the sky. The buzzards became doves and one of them lent me her wings. I flew with them happy and exhilarated throughout the night.

I think the dogs are finally gone.

Dec. 31, 12:10am
New Year's Eve was peaceful. I did a ritual I found in a book of African ceremonies. Poured some libations for my parents, burned my locks to the ancestors. Got deep with it. First time for me. I usually try and shake my ass on someone's dance floor. This was infinitely more fulfilling. I feel like I ... accomplished something. Like I really gave the direction of my life some serious thought and some positive energy. I feel focused. No "wooden nickels"—mamma's phrase for false things. Every time I went out for New Year's Eve before now, there would be this pressure to have a grand time, to get my money's worth, to drink, to kiss someone at midnight, to try and get laid ... all empty, all wooden nickels. And if any one part of that equation didn't come together just right, the disappointment would dampen my spirits for at least a week. What a way to start the New Year. Ain't nothing worse than starting the new year with a wack party. Right now, I feel uplifted. Energetic. I shoulda got hip to this ritual thing a while back. The flyest part was burning my locks. I don't need what they held any more.

Can't sit still. I'm gonna go walk it off.

* * *

Dante ended up at Zena's. It was close. It was trendy. At night the older women who hovered and jostled behind the bar during the day evaporated and beautiful multi-ethnic folk that spent their days as personal trainers, models and actresses took over their stations.

All the neighborhood black bourgeoisie were decorating Zena's barstools. Lost in boisterous New Year's revelry or quiet moments leaning close to someone special, or maybe someone who just became special a few hours before.

A slim brother with narrow glasses languished on a sofa, basking in the gleam from his lady's eyes. Her friends kept clamoring to stare at her left hand and the shiny, cluster of sparkles that Dante could see from across the room. She'd been crying happily, and Dante could see that too.

He got seated at the same corner table where he'd had his talk with Eva. He didn't feel the need to switch seats—to try to avoid the bad energy. He would override it. He'd grown.

He ordered a martini, then changed it to a hot chocolate.

New leaves everywhere.

He was still blowing on the hot chocolate when she floated into the empty seat across from him. He didn't look up. He could see her hands and they were more than recognizable. A cracked moonstone with a bluish tint decorated one of her fingers. That was new.

He didn't expect to see her. Not here. Not now. But when he thought about it, it made perfect sense.

She didn't speak, so they sat quiet and comfortable in the silence. She ordered a Kir Royale and sipped it slowly as her eyes watched him slurp his hot chocolate from a spoon.

She was amused by the look of it and her lips pulled into a tentative smile. He smiled back, knowing he was the brunt of the joke but feeling secure enough not to care. For a moment, he thought about telling her what he'd written about her in his journal but he didn't feel the need. In his heart it was settled— and the peace that brought him would dictate how they'd interact.

They both had barely a sip left in their glasses when he finally broke the silence.

"Thank you."

She froze with the champagne flute raised halfway to her lips. The moonstone caught the dim light and tossed it around playfully while her face drew into a question that she didn't think it was necessary to voice.

He answered her. "For the inspiration."

He didn't expect to have to explain himself.

A giddy laugh drifted over from a table by the window. Scented candles created invisible clouds of sweet smelling myrrh. A waitress in a close-fitting chocolate brown top breezed by with a tray of something that smelled like syrup, salt and bananas. Zena herself walked past the bar, pulling every eye as she went, then disappeared into the back.

When she finally responded, she looked Dante in the eye. Her voice was steady, making a statement more than asking a question, "A book?"

"Yeah."

She traced a lazy finger around the rim of her glass, then down the side. Picked up some condensation. Transferred the moisture to her tongue. Made sure he was watching her when she did. "Do I get a chapter?"

He smiled at her and for the first time in his life he felt like his smile was strong enough to pull light out of anyone who might glance his way. "What do you think?"

She didn't hesitate. "I think I should get two."

"Greedy." They laughed. Just a taste.

"So? ... " She looked at him.

"Later," he said. "Who am I?"

She was intrigued by the question. Like she was surprised and gratified that he asked it, but didn't quite know what to do with it. She took her last swallow of Kir Royale before she answered. He noticed that she let her tongue linger on the rim before she put the glass back on the table. She noticed him noticing.

"You tell me," she said.

He hadn't prepared an answer because he hadn't expected her to reflect his question back to him, but he opened his mouth and everything was right there, leaping off of his tongue and taking flight with his thoughts.

"I am Dante. King and queen of me. I am Dante. A writer. The shaper of my own destiny. I am Dante. A man no longer a boy. A man on the verge of the rest of his life. I am Dante and I am becoming the me that I want to be."

She considered. Shifted her weight. Used the candle to warm the tips of her fingers. Then she met his eyes. Her head was tilted to the side. She was wearing a slight frown. Finally she shook her head.

"You disagree?" he asked.

She nodded.

He wasn't as bothered as he expected to be.

He waited for her. When it came, it was a short sentence with a lot of power.

"You forgot the inferno."

He paused. "Dante's Inferno? Like the book?" he asked finally, lights and sparks leaping to life in his imagination like luminescent butterflies.

She smiled, ivory keys contrasting the dark shade painted on her lips. "Yeah," she said. "You conquered your inferno. So claim it."

He nodded back at her, trying not to show that her simple words had opened up floodgates inside him. He was blissfully set adrift on a whole new series of ideas about himself. He knew the next book he had to read. The next book he had to write. The next step he had to take. It was all coalescing instantly behind the glassy luster of his eyes.

"I am Dante. Conqueror of my inferno."

She raised her empty flute to salute his words. He clicked his empty mug against it with a smile. When her moonstone was resting on the table again the tension thickened. Potential wafted between them. He backed away from it, slid a twenty dollar bill onto the table and rose. "Thanks again," he said.

She stopped him with a hand on his thigh. "So? … " She looked up at him with her question mirrored in the sparkle of her eyes.

"The book? I'm going to call it *When Butterflies Kiss*." She nodded, then squeezed his leg. Just a little. Very subtle. Very appropriate … considering. He took her meaning, kissed her forehead lightly before he answered her. "That would be wonderful—luscious, plus decadent, times ten … but I need to just be with me for a while."

She let her hand drop slowly, exploring the fabric of his pants, even though he could tell his words had only made her want to tighten her grip. He expected her to try again but she must have recognized the new cadence of his voice. She smiled at him as he turned toward the door.

When Dante walked outside he could feel his breath fluttering happily inside him. He was just weeks away from a time when he could have never demurred on the pleasures of flesh. Especially hers. But he was rebuilding himself—better than ever. He entertained visions of the six million dollar man running in slow motion as he walked home.

Back at his apartment he pulled up his extended Sadé playlist and hit the "shuffle" button. Her music soothed him while he went to work on the monstrous task of making his apartment look presentable again.

When he was finally finished, and his apartment stopped looking and smelling like a garbage dump, he plugged his answering machine back in. Then he took one last look around the old digs he'd just imbued with new energy and opened his journal. He had to smile when he saw that the journal only had one blank, unlined page left. Right on time. He pulled out his red pen and scrawled hugely across the middle of it.

Jan. 1
Mom—
Today is my graduation day. Congratulate me.

Dante closed the journal, stared at the cliff and ocean on its cover, then put it in the wooden box that used to contain his locks. The box was resting beneath his window and when he looked up, he noticed that the sun was cracking brilliant orange and pink splits into the indigo sky hovering over the buildings around him. Sunrise. He'd been missing out on those recently.

Somehow he felt like this was the most important one he'd seen. The one he was meant to see.

He climbed out onto the fire escape despite the cold and sat, transfixed, as the sky and clouds above him cycled slowly through the most passionate colors in a master painter's palate and left the horizon looking like a streak of purplish pink velvet.

When the sky was finally pale blue and full of light, Dante felt the serenity in his chest reach its peak. He reached for the window and was about to climb back inside when he felt himself being watched. He turned to find a pair of greenish eyes staring. The Siamese cat was back. She was perched higher on the fire escape gazing down at him casually, as if she'd always been there, just waiting for him to notice.

The cat's mouth moved. Dante heard something, and to this day he swears he heard the cat say, "Congrats," before she smiled and melted away into the morning. Maybe. Maybe she just meowed.

Either way, that Siamese cat still materializes on his fire escape every so often and watches him. Whenever she does, Dante smiles … and thinks of his mother.

Biographies

Want to know who wrote which chapter? Following are our original 2001 bios from the first printing of *When Butterflies Kiss* along with a current update.

Chapter one: The Midnight Ocean of Moonlit Rivers
By SékouWrites (Male)
2001: SékouWrites is a Brooklyn-based writer of poetry, songs, articles, novels and whatever else he can get his mind around. He has published poetry, freelanced for entertainment venues including *VIBE, VIBE Online, True, New Word, Tafrija,* and *People* Online and currently serves as the senior writer of an Internet start-up, *blackfilm.com.* As a novelist, he is attempting to be one of the few African-American authors to break into the suspense thriller genre. Toward that end, he is currently shopping a suspense thriller to publishers and submitting the same to film production companies. When he's not scribbling something in red ink, or chasing the other writers in this collective to turn in their &#%@ chapter on time, he collects bad date stories.

Update: Since *When Butterflies Kiss,* SékouWrites has earned an MFA in Creative Writing, moved to Harlem and served as the managing editor of UPTOWN magazine. He is now a freelance writer and editor.

More at: **sekouwrites.com**

Chapter two: Dust
By Elizabeth Clara Brown (Female)
2001: Elizabeth Clara Brown received her MFA in Fiction from New York University, where she also taught undergraduate creative writing. She now spends her time writing stories with third-graders (who are much more fun than college kids) at a public school in Manhattan.

Update: Elizabeth Clara Brown currently lives in Japan. She is at work on her first novel.

Chapter three: Cats & Tambourines
By T'kalla (Male)
2001: Brooklyn-born T'kalla is one of the dark knights of the Renaissance Soul Movement gripping the planet. He is the Executive Director of *Meridian* magazine. A writer, poet, and music producer, he has just completed the Mango Room's self titled debut CD (Hardboiled/Blackbyrd Music) and is putting the last touches on his first volume of poetic prose, *Raising Sugarkane: Diary Of An Angel's Exile Into Flesh.*
Update: Poet, producer, playwright T'kalla is developing a feature film debut called *Boundless,* based on the writings of Shakespeare, Euripides and John Milton. It is a story of love, war and Eden.
More at: **myspace.com/tkalla**

Chapter four: Treasure the Savior
By Kiini Ibura Salaam (Female)
2001: Kiini Ibura Salaam is an artist and world traveler. Her fiction has appeared in *Fertile Ground, Dark Eros,* and *Dark Matter.* Her essays have been published in anthologies and magazines nationwide. She lives in Brooklyn.
Update: Since *When Butterflies Kiss,* Kiini Ibura Salaam has become a mother, spent a year in Oaxaca, Mexico, and obtained an MFA degree in Creative Writing. She has published a number of essays and short stories in various anthologies, literary magazines and online publications. She is currently working on her first novel, *Fate.* She continues to live in Brooklyn.
More at: **kiiniibura.com**

Chapter five: Wet Dreams
By Korby Marks (Male)
2001: Korby Marks is a Los Angeles-based filmmaker, screenwriter, poet and novelist. He has published poetry, had his filmwork featured in film festivals and is currently completing his first novel, *The Suicide Pilot*. This novel is an exploration of a man's struggle to overcome his addiction to sex and self-destructive behavior.

Update: Since *When Butterflies Kiss*, Korby Marks has taken the comic book world by storm. His first title, *Stormbringers*, featuring a team of African-American superheroes, dropped in the summer of 2007 and is available in comic book stores everywhere.

More at: **stormbringers.com**

Chapter six: Naked Truths
By Shange (Female)
2001: Previously published in a variety of literary magazines and anthologies, Shange completed an MS in Publishing in 1997 and launched Atlanta-based Silver Lion Press in 1999. While handling her business as publisher, she still finds time to write for various publications and consults and provides workshops on a variety of publishing subjects.

Update: Shange is now a freelance writer living in Santa Monica, CA.

Chapter seven: Flicker in the Night
By Kim Green (Female)
2001: Kim Green is a writer currently working on her first novel. She is the author of *On A Mission; Selected Poems and A History of the Last Poets*. She is also a freelance journalist and the owner of Veritas Communications, a full-service communications firm based in Tucson, Arizona.
Update: Kim Green has moved to Atlanta, Georgia, where she is finishing up her first novel. In the meantime, she authored the controversial *Life Is Not A Fairytale* with Fantasia Barrino (2004 *American Idol* winner), which was a best selling book and was made into a Lifetime Television movie. Kim is also doing commercial creative writing.
More at: **kimgreenwords.com**

Chapter eight: Moments of Truth
By Mariahadessa Ekere Tallie (Female)
2001: Poet, writer, journalist, New Yorker Mariahadessa Ekere Tallie's work has appeared in publications in the United States and France. She is one of nine poets featured in the anthology *Listen Up!* (One World/Ballantine).
Update: Since *When Butterflies Kiss*, Ekere received her MFA from Mills College. She has taught English and creative writing in London, Amsterdam, Rundu, New York and Chicago and wandered joyously through more cities than she will admit. She muses on writing, travel, life, and motherhood on her website.
More at: **ekeretallie.com**

Chapter nine: Sour and Sweet
By Natasha Tarpley (Female)

2001: Natasha Tarpley is the author of the anthology, *Testimony: Young African Americans on Self-Discovery and Black Identity* (Beacon) and a family memoir, *Girl in the Mirror: Three Generations of Black Women in Motion* (Beacon). Ms. Tarpley has also written several books for children including, *I Love My Hair!* (Little, Brown & Co.) and *Bippity-Bop Barbershop!* (forthcoming from Little, Brown in 2002). Ms. Tarpley lives in New York City.
Update: No update available.

Chapter ten: On Top of the Game
By Tish Benson (Female)

2001: Texas-born writer and performer Tish Benson currently lives in Brooklyn, New York. A New York Foundation for the Arts Fellowship Recipient in play writing, her verses have been installed at The Aldrich Museum's "NO DOUBT" exhibition. She has been published in magazines and books including: *Listen Up!*, *In The Tradition: An Anthology of Young Black Writers*, *Long Shot Magazine* and *Verses that Hurt: Pleasure and Pain* from the Poemfone Poets. A 1999 MFA graduate from NYU in Dramatic Writing, her plays have included a one-woman show ("Boxed") and several others that revolve around a mythical town in Texas. Tish Benson's most recent work includes a collection of short stories and poems as well as "Thick Heat" a tele-play which will be aired on LIFETIME in May of 2001.
Update: Tish Benson has had an awakening and become "Turah." In this divine manifestation of the goddess she blesses her godchildren with the first eye of the ancients and she

continues to write with the knowing ways opened—serving up performance art every day and every night.

Chapter eleven: *C'est La Vie*
Also by SékouWrites

Frequently Asked Questions

Here are a few of the questions that I get asked most frequently about *When Butterflies Kiss*. If you're hosting a book club meeting (and I hope you are) you can use these questions as a point of departure to discuss the novel.

Also, you should explore the question of how your book club would choose to write a serial story. Try it. I've conducted serial writing seminars for both elementary school and college students—the results are never the same. Try your hand at it, discuss the process and then you'll have an even better understanding of how *When Butterflies Kiss* was created.

YOU EDITED *WHEN BUTTERFLIES KISS*. WHAT DOES THAT MEAN?

Essentially, it was my brainchild. After I had the idea for creating an African-American serial novel. I made a list of my writing dream team and I went knocking on doors—or, more literally, sending emails. I did have a few major, well-known writers in mind but there were often hurdles, like agents, managers, publicists, hefty writing fees and often a reluctance to attach their name to a somewhat nebulous project. After a few rounds of that, I decided to follow my heart and pick up-and-coming writers who could benefit from the exposure. Thankfully, I was part of a writing group at the time so I culled most of my writers from there.

I also edited each chapter as it was turned in for both content and continuity and I kept a running list of "loose ends" that I would forward to each new writer when I sent them the chapters preceding the one they were supposed to write. I did this so that I would not have to tie up all of the loose ends in the final chapter.

Once the book was published, I was the front man, so to speak. I envisioned all ten of the writers traveling to every book signing at first but I quickly realized how unrealistic and logistically challenging that expectation was. Besides, as one of the writers explained to me at the time, it was really "my" book. I was the creator, editor and organizer. I was the most passionate about it. I was the most willing to endure whatever discomforts necessary to promote the book. And I was willing to spend just about every penny of my money to promote *Butterflies*. And, trust me, I did.

Speaking of money, people always ask about the financial arrangements. That's kind of like asking what someone's salary is, but because it often comes up, it's worth a mention.

Silver Lion Press used a fiction anthology template for the book, which means that, as the editor, I was promised a royalty rate if the book sold enough copies to break even on the publishing costs. Like many first time authors, I never reached that particular milestone. The royalty was offered because, as with a fiction anthology, the workload of the editor is much different than that of a contributing writer. The other nine writers each signed individual work-for-hire contracts with Silver Lion Press, meaning that they were promised a flat fee to contribute one chapter of the novel and to hopefully help promote it every once in a while.

As is the case with many small presses, no advance was offered to me, so I helped fund the various book events out of my pocket. All told, I didn't make any money on the first edition the book, but I'd like to think that I could have if it had remained in print longer. Hopefully, the second edition will fare better.

HOW WAS THE BOOK CREATED?

Imagine a group of ten writers sitting in the same room, at the same table. Imagine them having a conversation about the fact that they are about to create a novel and that each of them is going to write a chapter of it. Imagine them deciding who is going to write first, who is going to write second, etcetera. Now, imagine that they all discuss each chapter after they complete it and share ideas for the next chapter.

If that's what you envision when you think about how *When Butterflies Kiss* was created, you're wrong.

What I just described is a collaborative novel. That's a novel where two or more authors work together to create a novel.

So, what exactly is a serial novel? The first distinguishing characteristic of a serial novel is the fact that each writer contributes a chapter to the story independently, without influence from the other authors. The second distinguishing characteristic of a serial novel is having large group of contributing writers; usually ten or more.

In the case of *When Butterflies Kiss* many of the ten writers who contributed to the story have never met or spoken to each other. In fact, all ten of us have never been in the same room.

When I was in high school, I didn't know about serial novels yet, but I was the kid who always ripped out a sheet of notebook paper, wrote the beginning of a short story on it and passed it around the room. When the sheet of paper made its way back to me, I was always thrilled and surprised by what kind of story had evolved.

Of course, this being high school, you can easily imagine that most of our classroom tales ended up very close to pornographic but, there was also depth and nuance in the prose as well. The memories of that childhood habit never left me. One day, I promised myself, I'd do the same with a group of talented writers.

Many years (and moves) later, I wrote what I intended to be the first chapter of a full fledged serial novel and passed it on to one of my writer friends. She read my chapter and added her chapter on behind it. Once I edited her chapter, I sent both chapter one and chapter two on to the third writer, who added his chapter based on the first two. After the first three chapters were compete, I unexpectedly ended up with a publishing deal from Silver Lion Press and they came on board to help shepherd the project to completion.

Each writer was able to see the chapters that came before theirs but not the chapters that came after. Although I edited the chapters for continuity as we went along, I never suggested an overarching storyline. I simply sent an introductory note to each writer explaining that my intention was to create an erotic serial novel. I chose this general subject matter because I was hoping the sexual content would make it an easier sell in the marketplace. Plus, erotic anthologies were popular at the time. It was not meant to be though.

Some of the writers forgot my instructions, some of them didn't read my note, some of them were led in a different direction by the prose and, even more important, I neglected to take into consideration the fact that every person's interpretation of what "erotic" means is different. So, for each chapter where eroticism is evident, the way it's presented is a reflection of that particular writer's take on it.

What astounded me (and what I hope will please you) is the strong theme of rebirth and renewal that developed within this work of fiction. The nameless male character I introduced in chapter one, gradually and profoundly filled out the pages upon which he was written and grew into a man who we want to root for, a man who wants to make himself better.

Male introspection and self-discovery are rare themes in the media, especially in fiction. Even less so when it comes to African-American men. I could not have imagined a better outcome for my little science project. The end product is certainly more emotionally resonant than the erotic love story I originally intended.

DID YOU MAKE ANY CHANGES FOR THIS SECOND EDITION?

Indeed, I did. Aside from a new cover, new dedication, lengthy introduction, chapter re-ordering and a list of frequently asked questions, I also had the entire manuscript copy edited and made changes throughout. Mostly, I made updates to make the book seem less dated.

There was a telephone booth conversation, for example, that got replaced with a cell phone call; using a phone booth in this day and age is almost unheard of. Likewise, I deleted a reference to Monica Lewisnsky; although that scandal was fairly topical in 2001, it's ancient history now and I wanted the novel to feel current.

I also made some editorial changes to make the story read better. My editing eye has changed a bit over the years. Most notably, I deleted all instances of the N-word. In the original version, the N-word made several appearances, with different spellings. I've never been comfortable with that, since I don't believe in using the N-word at all and, for the second edition, I decided to take that word out.

ARE THERE ANY OTHER SERIAL NOVELS?

The first serial novel that I'm aware of was created in the 1930s when Agatha Christie along with several mystery writing giants of her era decided to create a single novel with each of them writing independent chapters. The novel that resulted, *The Floating Admiral,* was a huge success.

The next serial novel in America's history was *Naked Came the Stranger*, which was supposedly written by a Connecticut housewife named Penelope Ashe but was in reality written by twenty-five *Newsday* journalists. It was published in 1969 as an attempt by the authors to prove that a novel brimming with sex would sell—no matter how poorly-written. It worked, of course.

The strong sales of *Naked Came the Stranger* were not lost on Carl Hiaasen, a Florida-based journalist and author. In 1995, Hiaasen and some of his co-workers at the *Miami Herald* began a serial story that ran in the *Miami Herald's Tropic* magazine, one chapter per week. Reader response was so great that Ballantine Books picked up the rights and published what came to be known as *Naked Came the Manatee* and it went on to reach *The New York Times* bestseller list. The thirteen co-authors, including Elmore Leonard and Tananarive Due, did not hide behind a pseudonym or intentionally try to write a bad book; their manuscript was a deftly crafted mystery spoof.

A number of serial novels have appeared on bookshelves since then. Most have fallen into the mystery genre, like *Naked Came the Phoenix, Natural Suspect* and *Like a Charm*. There are several non-mystery themed serials novels, however, like *The Putt at the End of World* and *Finbar's Hotel*.

My goal with *When Butterflies Kiss* was to create the very first serial novel written by African-American writers. As far as I know, we succeeded, which would make this book the first (and only) of its kind. Save a copy for your grandkids.

HOW WERE THE WRITERS CHOSEN?

When planning *When Butterflies Kiss*, I selected writers I knew personally (and who I knew could throw down, writing-wise). Some of those writers knew each other, others did not. Also, I did not allow myself to be confined by geographic location. While most of my writers were based in New York at the time, not all of them were. One writer lived in Los Angeles, for example, while another wrote most of his chapter from London, England. We just moved the manuscript around via email.

Had I to do it over again, though, the dispassionate distance inherent in working with writers you do not know probably makes things easier. I butted heads with each of the co-writers over some edit or another during the course of creating *When Butterflies Kiss*. Don't think for a second that it was all smooth sailing.

When you get to the bios at the end of the book, you will notice that I wrote both the first and the final chapter. I did this because I wanted to start the story off and ultimately I thought it should fall to me to tie up all the loose ends. As any serial novel enthusiast will tell you, the final chapter of a serial novel is the clean-up chapter. It's the biggest challenge of the whole book because you have to tie up all the loose ends for the reader.

It was also my intention to alternate genders—male writer, female writer, etcetera. The idea being (at the time) that each writer would write from the perspective of their own gender, i.e. the male writers would write about the character that came to be named Dante and the female writers would write about his love interest, a character named Eliza. Again, I was expecting to end up with an erotic love story.

I was able to switch genders three times and then I ran out of male writers in my immediate circle. The rest of the writers of *When Butterflies Kiss* were women. Not that it mattered—they are talented enough to write from the perspective of any character.

Speaking of which, isn't it interesting (and telling) that with seven women and three men, *When Butterflies Kiss* ended up being about the spirit of a man, not a woman?

HOW LONG DID IT TAKE TO CREATE THE BOOK?

In terms of timeline, the publisher and I requested that each new chapter be written in one week.

Yeah, okay, I suppose that was a bit ambitious, but *Naked Came the Manatee* had accomplished the same successfully so I thought we could, too. The *Manatee* writers, of course, were all newspaper journalists, used to fast writing and tight deadlines. My writers took their time. And not all of them were fiction writers, *per se*. At least two of my writers were spoken word artists (performance poets), a field of expression that is typically cultured by creative inspiration, not deadlines.

We planned to produce *When Butterflies Kiss* in two months. Instead, it took two years.

DID YOU HAVE ANY RULES FOR THE WRITERS?

I made a point of letting the writers do whatever they wanted, which is why the chapters and themes are so varied. I think that made for a more interesting read.

There is one rule that applies to serial novel production, though: Don't rearrange the chapters. We broke that rule with the first edition of *When Butterflies Kiss*, moving two chapters out of sequence to make the novel read more fluidly.

In this second edition of *When Butterflies Kiss*, the chapters appear in the order that they were originally written. I changed the sequence back because I think that's part of the fun, to see what each writer had to work with and where they took the story from there. I wanted you, the reader, to experience the story the way the writers did. That's the thrill of serial writing.

So, if someone who has the first edition of *When Butterflies Kiss* is looking over your shoulder claiming you got a bootleg copy because the chapters are out of order, set them straight for me. It's the second edition, not the first, which has the chapters printed in their original order.

HOW IMPORTANT WAS EDITING IN THE OVERALL PROCESS?

Editing was key. Paramount really. Any time you have ten people talking about anything, you're bound to have trouble (even if it's just what to get on the pizza). With a serial novel, multiply that by twenty.

Case in point. In chapter one, the main character mentions driving to someone's house, which means he owns (or has access to) a car. For the rest of the novel, however, not a single writer made use of that car. They all had this character riding the bus, walking, taking the train and traveling by any means, expect driving. I suppose that's because most of the *When Butterflies Kiss* co-writers have ties to New York City and using a car in New York if often considered superfluous. To improve the experience for the reader, though, I needed to eliminate such an obvious hiccup, so I went back into chapter one and edited the car out of the story. I didn't want readers wondering why he wasn't driving his car.

I had to make similar edits throughout the other chapters. One of the writers, for example, wrote a provocative sexual scene. A writer who came later didn't want to reference the episode because she didn't necessarily think it fit the story. I respected her opinion but I didn't want the reader's experience to be diminished by feeling like something huge had happened that was never mentioned again. I asked (more like begged) her to add at least a sentence about the episode to maintain continuity.

She added exactly one sentence. I had to laugh. Such is the nature of the beast. Each author interacts with the work and the characters differently. And even I, as the editor, can't change that.

WAS IT HARD TO LET THE CHARACTERS GO AFTER YOU CREATED THEM?

One of the wonderful things about writing a novel is being able to live with your characters for a long time; to sit with them and let them grow inside of you. A unique challenge of writing a serial novel is to be able to let the characters go after you work with them.

I was dismayed as early as chapter two because the author of that chapter did not take the story where I expected it to go. What I expected was a love story between the two characters in chapter one. I just assumed the other writers would create a hot, sexy love story that ended with these characters living happily ever after.

Not so much.

The author of chapter two thought it would be interesting to have the woman's interpretation of the set of events be completely different than the man's perspective of those same events. And isn't that just like real life, which makes the story that much more authentic?

Still, I realized right then that I had to take a deep breath and let go of my preconceived notions of what the plot would turn out to be.

WHY ONLY TEN WRITERS?

It was hard enough with ten writers. One more writer might have driven us up the wall. To tell the truth, we had planned to go for eleven or twelve writers but when I read chapter ten, I couldn't help myself. Suddenly, I knew what *When Butterflies Kiss* was about and how to end it. I wrote the final chapter in one big burst of energy.

Now that I've completed my MFA in creative writing, I know that most of my teachers and fellow students would refer to that final chapter (and most of the book) as being overwritten. For me, though, that only serves as a reminder that the tastes of the literary elite are not the tastes of mass-market consumers. What I'm hoping is that *When Butterflies Kiss* will eventually find a place somewhere in between—accessible enough to sell in the mass market but literary enough to be respected. Of course, that's up to you.

Ten writers was just right for us. Next time—if there is a next time—I'll probably use even fewer than that.

WHAT KIND OF FEEDBACK HAVE YOU GOTTEN?

I've had people tell me that *When Butterflies Kiss* could have been written by one person. Others have told me it read like an anthology of short stories about a man named Dante. I can say that in all of the other serial novels I've read there is always at least a slight break from chapter to chapter in terms of voice, tone and direction. Is that a good thing? I suppose that's up to you.

The best compliment I've gotten about *When Butterflies Kiss*? A few brothers told me that the book had changed the way they interacted with women for the better. I was humbled. And for that type of impact to come from this unscripted book, without us planning to write anything profound, was magical. I feel blessed to be a part of something so grand. That's part of why I decided to put this book back into print.

Reader's Guide

ARE YOU THE REAL DANTE?

Since I knew each of the writers, I could sometimes see glimpses of their actual lives in the evolving narrative. And, since Dante (the protagonist) ended up being a sensitive, New York-based black male writer with dreadlocks, readers everywhere assumed that Dante was really me, which makes for interesting commentary about how readers interact with fiction.

I couldn't actually *be* Dante because that would have required each of my nine co-writers to know me well enough to write about the intimate details of my personal life. Not so much. I will, however, admit that there are some uncanny similarities between Dante and myself (aside from the obvious). And, yes, my two chapters are based on my life experiences. How literal they are, I won't say. Have to leave something to the imagination.

One of my goals with chapter one was to write about a man who was introspective to the point that his internal dialogue was sometimes completely contradictory to his external actions. I waned a sensitive, thoughtful black man who, even though he might be chasing skirts, is conflicted about it. I don't often seen men like that in fiction, so I wanted to create one. I suppose the rest of the writers took my cue.

WHO IS DANTE TALKING TO AT ZENA'S IN THE FINAL CHAPTER? WHY DON'T YOU TELL THE READER WHO SHE IS?

By the time readers reach the end of the novel, Dante has interacted with a number of women, so I wrote that scene in such a way so that each individual reader could insert the woman who they felt should be there.

I also wanted to give readers a little mystery; a question mark that would remain long after the book had been put down. What I've found though is that *sometimes* people ask me which woman was in the final chapter but more often than not, readers have simply decided for themselves who was there and don't feel the need to ask.

The interesting thing about *When Butterflies Kiss* is that—because it was not written collaboratively—I can't speak to the book as a whole. Remember that each successive chapter was as much a surprise to me as it was to you. I had no idea what to expect, so my interaction with the book as a whole is very much like yours. I can tell you all about my intentions in the two chapters I wrote, but if I tell you my interpretation of the other nine chapters, I'll just be speculating. I have a slight advantage because there were at least one or two book signings where several co-writers were present so I got to hear them talk about what their intentions were. But not much. Mostly we were signing books and posing for pictures. That said, I do have a personal interpretation of the book as a whole. But it is no more accurate than your interpretation. *When Butterflies Kiss* is subjective art at its best.

That said, based on my synthesis of the book as a whole, I wrote the final chapter thinking that no one is sitting with him at Zena's; that the other seat at his table is empty.

For me, he's talking to Treasure (TreeLawn) but I don't believe that Treasure exists. Not in the flesh and blood world, anyway. I think Treasure is an expression of Dante's internal self. Just like the dogs are a manifestation of his darker, haunted nature, Treasure represents the opposite of that within him—the good angel on his shoulder, so to speak.

Throughout the novel Treasure does (and knows) some things that are not altogether ordinary and magic always seems to follow in her wake. Plus, we never see her interact with anyone except Dante. Well, there is that one scene in chapter four where an aggressive man is accosting her, but it seems to me that particular man is just a different personification of Dante's dogs. The aggressive man and the dogs seem to have the same energy, as do Treasure and the motherly Siamese cat. Treasure pops up throughout the novel and tries to put Dante back on track. That seems to be her sole purpose. So, I think she's a part of his mind, not a part of the brick and mortar world.

That would mean, by extension, that Dante sabotages any possibility of intimacy by scattering panties throughout his apartment or perhaps just by neglecting to collect the ones that his various conquests have left behind. Strange, I'll admit. But I've heard of stranger things. And for someone who was molested as a child, it might not be too far off the mark for Dante.

If you apply my theory throughout the book, it would also mean that when we see Dante having sex with Treasure that he is simply masturbating. This is not much of a stretch for Dante, and it falls in line with the idea of Treasure protecting him; if he's masturbating, that means he's not out there messing around with all these women who give him so many woes.

So, back to the lecture at hand. My interpretation? At Zena's, Dante is telling Treasure that he no longer needs her. He's matured to the place where he can stand on his own, without her. I think he's having a drink alone, thinking things through and when she tempts him with sex, she is testing him—

seeing if he will pick up the phone and start calling women to arrange a sexual rendezvous or be strong enough to stand alone.

After the end of this novel, I would not expect Dante to ever see Treasure again unless he fell deep into despair—in which case, I think she would reappear.

So, that's my answer: I wrote my chapter thinking that the chair at Zena's is empty. But that's only my answer.

Who do *you* think is sitting with Dante?

IS MALIK A MALIGNANT PERSON OR A TRUE FRIEND WHO PRACTICES TOUGH LOVE?

Again, we never had a group discussion as writers about the character arcs or themes. I can't say any better than you can what Malik's motives are. I can tell you that I always considered Malik a toxic person, as evidenced by what I wrote in my final chapter.

Once, however, at a book club meeting in Brooklyn, I was surprised to find that most of those assembled were of the opinion that Malik was a real friend who was trying to shock Dante onto the right path. This book club refused to believe that Malik slept with Sheron. Instead, they thought Malik lied about having sex with Sheron in order to push Dante away from a woman he knew would bring Dante down—even if it cost their friendship.

I was fascinated by this perspective and, although I still tend to think Malik was threatened by Dante's growth, I can easily see how someone might think otherwise.

Strange as it sounds, I've heard of people having sex with a woman just to prove to someone else that the woman in question is a bad apple. That might not be what you or I would do, but I've heard stories. Malik could be that type of person.

WHERE DID MR. CRISSER COME FROM?

I felt like Dante needed some type of trauma to help explain (not excuse) his bad behavior with women. Something deep-seated and dark that bound him and Malik together and affected Dante in ways he had yet to realize. It was my search for such an occurrence, as well as a desire to revisit Dante's youth, that inspired Mr. Crisser.

I've had a few readers tell me that it was hard for them to read that scene. Good. That means I'm doing my job as a writer.

Now, as to my rationale ... here is another interesting point of discussion. Some of the book clubs I've talked to appreciated the Mr. Crisser episode because it explained Dante's behavior, at least partially.

On the other hand, more than a few women (no men, so far) have told me that they felt cheated by Mr. Crisser. Why? Because they say that there are men who act irresponsibly with women all the time and most of them don't have some harrowing childhood experience to blame it on. To these women, Mr. Crisser felt like a cheat, an easy out. They wanted me to let Dante overcome his behavior after coming to terms with the fact that he was a user of women.

It is a very interesting perspective and one that makes me consider whether or not I would write that chapter a different way if I were to do it over.

It also opens the door to discuss Dante. *Was* he a user of women? Or a sensitive man with an easily confused heart? You can tell from both of my chapters what I think the answer is. I think Dante loves women. And I think his creative-writer-self lives for and thrives off of romance. Did he hurt women? Absolutely. But I think, in his way, that Dante genuinely loved (and fell for) each of them and didn't mean to cause them harm.

WHAT DOES THE TITLE OF THE BOOK MEAN?

Many readers think that the title, *When Butterflies Kiss*, was chosen after the book was written and that it refers to some aspect of the story. Not so. The title actually preceded the creation of the novel.

The title in this case is a description of what the novel is. At least, to me. I think this serial novel is the sum of what happens when writers (or creative spirits, or butterflies) come together (or work in tandem, or kiss).

That's the whole story. It's just that the writers on this project were so marvelously talented that they were able to weave that title, or threads of it, into the novel, making you feel like the title could have easily been extracted from the text, when it was actually the other way around.

Interesting side note. My original title was *A Gathering of Obsidian-Drenched Velvet Butterflies*, which the publisher and I eventually deemed too dense. *When Butterflies Kiss* felt perfect.

WHAT DOES THE THEME OF WATER THROUGHOUT THE TEXT REPRESENT?

Trick question. We never discussed our literary intentions as a group. There was no overarching plan. I wasn't even aware of the water theme until an astute woman in a book club meeting asked me about it. I have to credit the emergence of this theme and (others like it) to the talent of the co-writers.

I gave the female character in chapter one a very provocative nickname related to large bodies of water. After that, I think water kept making cameos throughout the work because the other writers consciously or subconsciously chose to continue it. Considering the fluid nature of Dante's interactions with women, I think it fits.

WHAT ROLE DOES ELIZA SERVE IN DANTE'S GROWTH?

The answer to this question — like the others listed here — is entirely subjective. I only include it because I happen to have an opinion on the subject. Even though Eliza fades out before the end of the novel I think she plays a significant role. To me, Eliza is Dante's emotional twin. I think Eliza completes her arc of loving the wrong people for the wrong reasons much more quickly than Dante does and gives Dante a mirror by which to measure his actions with the opposite sex. Dante is too confused by his competing loves (lusts?) to make that connection but in my opinion it exists. Which leads us to the next question.

IS DANTE HEALED AT THE END OF THE NOVEL; HAS HE FOUND HIS WAY?

I'm not going to weigh in on this one. Find a friend who's read *When Butterflies Kiss* and talk it out. I will say that there are a number of reasons that you could cite to make the argument either way. And, of course, there is no wrong answer. I won't influence your opinion on the matter by giving mine.

WHAT IS IT ABOUT DANTE'S INTERACTIONS WITH WOMEN THAT MAKES SOME MALE READERS OF *WHEN BUTTERFLIES KISS* DECIDE TO TREAT THE WOMEN IN THEIR LIFE BETTER?

I admit that I'm not sure what it is about *When Butterflies Kiss* that affects some black men in this way, but I'm very interested in hearing from you about why you think this is so. In the interim, I've asked someone who is qualified to weigh in on the issue.

Dr. H. Jean Wright, II is a Philadelphia-based psychologist whom I meet at one of my first *When Butterflies Kiss* book signings. Over the years, his support, insight, and encouragement have been invaluable and we have collaborated on a number of projects revolving around black male empowerment, including Black Men on Black Love, which you'll read more about shortly. Here is his opinion of the book.

Dr. H Jean:

"*When Butterflies Kiss* takes the reader on a spirited journey along the twin paths of psychological intrigue and physical adventure. Readers will find themselves unwittingly mapping out their own psychological itinerary right along with the protagonist as he struggles to make sense of his conflicting emotions. As with any psychological journey, the goal is not simply to find self, but also to be able to accept and love the self we discover, and this book will challenge readers to do both. Readers will also find themselves reminiscing about their best life experiences as well as considering what sexual fantasies they have yet to fulfill. In the end, readers will be glad they embarked upon the journey and, more important, feel good about where they came to rest."

This small collection of questions is by no means a comprehensive list. It is merely a framework for your conversations with friends, lovers, or book club members. I've found that the deeper you dig with this book, the more you find worth unearthing. And that's not ego; it's a nod to the very talented writers who came together to make my vision of an African-American serial novel come together better than I could have imagined.

Before I go, I just have to remind you to come up with your own answers about *When Butterflies Kiss* because even though your answers might be different from mine, the funny this is, we're both right.

* * *

If you enjoyed the theme of black male empowerment that was present in *When Butterflies Kiss*, you may be interested in some similarly themed works book that are in development. Please subscribe to the email list to be notified about my upcoming projects and release dates. Thank you!

Subscribe at: www.sekouwrites.com